The Year of the Zinc Penny

The Year of the Zinc Penny

Rick DeMarinis

SEVEN STORIES PRESS
New York • London • Toronto • Melbourne

First Seven Stories Press Edition October 2004

Seven Stories Press
140 Watts Street
New York, NY 10013
www.sevenstories.com

IN CANADA

Publishers Group Canada, 250A Carlton Street, Toronto, ON M5A 2L1

IN THE UK

Turnaround Publisher Services Ltd., Unit 3,
Olympia Trading Estate, Coburg Road, Wood Green, London N22 6TZ

IN AUSTRALIA

Palgrave Macmillan, 627 Chapel Street, South Yarra VIC 3141

LIBRARY OF CONGRESS CATALOGING-IN-PUBLICATION DATA

DeMarinis, Rick, 1934-
The year of the zinc penny : a novel / Rick DeMarinis.— 1st pbk. ed.
p. cm.
ISBN 1-58322-638-9 (pbk. : alk. paper)
1. Boys—Fiction. 2. Stepfathers—Fiction. 3. Shortwave radio—Fiction.
4. Mothers and sons—Fiction. 5. Los Angeles (Calif.)—Fiction. I. Title.

PS3554.E4554Y44 2004
813'.54—dc22
2004016563

Book design by India Amos

9 8 7 6 5 4 3 2 1

Printed in Canada

The Year of the Zinc Penny

My first night in the foster home, a boy named Sylvester Snell decided that I belonged to him. He had a dead, unblinking gaze that gave his words full authority. There was no choice in the matter. But I didn't understand what he meant until he made four of us smaller boys bend over in front of him so that he could pick a favorite. When he began yanking down our pajamas, I yelled. I raised such a storm that the lady who owned the house, Mrs. Ryerson, came into the bedroom and clubbed Sylvester on the back of the head with her thick red hand. "It's nearly Christmas, you warped cornholer," she said. "Can't you keep your drawers up for the holidays?"

Mrs. Ryerson knew all about Sylvester, but she had nowhere else to keep him. He was a fox, in among the chickens. I wanted to tell her that she could put him down in the basement where he could be chained to the plumbing, but I was already getting dangerously significant glances from Sylvester for having yelled for help and didn't dare open my mouth again. As soon as Mrs. Ryerson left, Sylvester would reestablish his authority over the rest of us boys, and so my job now was to become anonymous.

Becoming anonymous was my special project that year. I had ordinary looks anyway and began to believe that I could make myself even more ordinary-looking so that I could blend in anywhere. It was a skill that would often come in handy. But on that particular night, the first of three that I'd have to spend in the care of foster parents because my own parents along with my Uncle Gerald had gotten themselves jailed for assaulting a police officer, I could only pray that Sylvester Snell would pick someone else. He did. He didn't care about pointless revenge.

He only wanted his way. For all his sharp ferocity, he had a stupid, baleful cast to his eyes that originated in his limited powers of memory and analytical thought. He was an animal that only happened to walk upright on two legs and express itself in crude English. Sometime after the lights were turned out, I heard whimpering. Sylvester had found a boy who was either too scared or too simple-minded to yell for help. I was so grateful that my prayer had been answered that I said another one for the whimpering boy.

Sylvester must have been twelve or thirteen years old, but he had the hard, whipcord muscles of a thirty-year-old stonemason. He had kinky gray hair, stiff as iron mesh. His eyes were also gray and they had an empty-minded stare that could make normal eyes blink or turn away. His homely, grayish face had a wolf-like elongation to it. His teeth were tapered, as if deliberately filed to deadly points, and the mouth that held them was lipless. He had long fuzzy ears, like a fox's. One of his ears, the left, had a hard nub of fuzzless cartilage sticking up from the top of it. It looked like a dried-up little toe. Years later I learned that this growth had a traditional name. It was called the "Devil's Hook" and was considered one of the more dependable signs of evil by people in the Middle Ages. Whenever I had nightmares about the devil coming for my soul, it was always lipless, dog-toothed Sylvester Snell with yellow horns and hooked ear.

I was too scared to sleep that night, even though Sylvester had decided to leave me alone. And when I did fall asleep sometime after dawn, I wet the bed. It was a major humiliation. At ten years old I was beyond the permissible age of nocturnal accident. Since I'd stayed up most of the night, on alert, the little sleep I got was profound, too profound to respond to emergency signals from the bladder. I tried to camouflage the disaster by making my bed before the others got up and by hiding my pungent pajamas under it. But the room was full of the rank odor and soon all the boys began to snicker, greatly pleased that someone besides them had been reduced to bed-wetting. Sylvester Snell, who found no amusement in anything, was the only one who didn't laugh at me.

↓

The last time I'd wet the bed was four years earlier, when I was six. I'd been sent to live with my grandparents in Montana after my mother's divorce from my father. It was a prairie house, wind-blasted on a butte above the protected town. The wind was constant and always blew at gale force. The town itself was in a river valley and its many hardwood trees, along with the low-lying butte that ran along its north edge, shielded it from the wind. No one lived on the butte except my grandparents. My grandfather claimed he liked to see the weather coming. He said he liked the sound of the wind in the eaves. Driving through town he would scoff at the rows of neat maples and elms, saying that they were not native to this land.

I was not native to that land, either. The high plains of north-central Montana scared me. There was too much sky. The horizon was so far away you were convinced you could see the curvature of the earth on a clear day. It was like seeing a horrendous truth underlying what had been a comfortable deception. My grand-father scared me, too. He was a big, angular man who seemed carved out of granite. He'd been a railroad man all his life until a crippling accident forced him to retire. Both his knees were jointless bone, fused solid. He moved in a slow, straight-legged shuffle, like Frankenstein's monster. Grandmother had to put his pants and shoes on every morning and take them off at night. He raised and lowered himself by means of thick cherry-wood canes with huge red rubber tips. His pale arms were heavily muscled from this difficult exercise.

He never spoke to me or to anyone else. He made statements whether anyone was within earshot or not. He would say, "Supper," and if Grandmother was in the house she'd release a long sigh and go into the kitchen. If he said, "Big blow a-comin', hey?" it didn't mean he wanted to discuss the weather. It meant the tomatoes had to be covered or the shutters closed. Never, to my knowledge, did he engage anyone in conversation. I suppose it came from the years he spent shouting one-way instructions over the roar and clang of engines and freight cars.

They were Norwegians and could not pronounce my Italian name properly. "Napoli" came out "Nappy Lee." Trygve Soren Napoli, me. They didn't like me much and I can't blame them. I was angry and resentful after my mother left me with them. I was an Italian from New York City and knew how to throw my weight around, even though I was only six. But they were not much impressed by my bullying. It soon became clear to me that they held the upper hand. If I refused to eat Norwegian food, they did not mind. After my two-day hunger strike I was ready to eat anything, including their pickled fish and flat, papery bread. And when I began to wet the bed regularly, my grandmother solved the problem with electric sheets. I shocked myself awake so many times I began to fear sleep. I'd lie awake for hours, inventing another life for myself.

Fear became the single dynamic that formed my world in the four years I stayed with my grandparents. In deference to the religion of my father's family, I was sent to the Catholic school in town where the pedagogical philosophy was Education Through Fear. Because fear was the most powerful force the children knew, they used it against one another. The bullies were merciless. The playground was a stage where sadistic dramas were played out daily. The "games" only gave formal sanction to the arm-twists, kicks, and punches. The priest who watched over us was expert in looking the other way. When a boy wept the priest would instruct him in what it took to be a man in this world. He believed strongly in the Old Testament and took the New Testament with a grain of salt. In his view, the spirit that governed the world was Punishment. "Retaliate in kind," he said, "or slink away like a miserable dog. The choice is yours."

↯

I was never aware of having choices. When I was sent to Los Angeles, it was as abrupt as every other major event in my life. My mother had remarried without notice and I was to join her. My stiff-kneed grandfather brought me to her. We rode the Great Northern to Seattle and the Northern Pacific to Los Angeles. He had to be lifted aboard the trains by two conductors. He didn't thank them, but acted as if they were part of the inconvenience. He spoke fewer than a dozen words during the entire trip. I didn't care. I pressed my face against the window of the coach and watched the magical transformation of the world, from flat brown endless fields patched with snow to dark mountains heavy with timber. I saw cities with tall white buildings rise into the blue Pacific sky. And I saw the ocean, like the bright rippling skin of an immense animal, curving out to the end of the world. For three days I forgot to be afraid.

But after only a week in Los Angeles, I found myself in Mrs. Ryerson's foster home. My fear, which had lost my scent and had allowed me a few days of freedom, moved against me with crushing weight. It flattened my spirit; it made me a zombie. My face in the mirror was only a face. It could be anyone. It was a face in a crowd, instantly forgettable. I needed this anonymity but my unusual name ruined it. My great desire was to adopt an anonymous American name that did not raise eyebrows. "Charles Jones" was typical of the names I wished for myself. If I was "Charles Jones" my fear would lose track of me.

I want one man to climb that hill and toss a grenade into the Jap machine gun nest.

I'll go, Sergeant.

Again, Charlie? You went last time, remember? You were wounded badly. Take a good look at Charlie Jones, boys. Here is a real hero.

Brief fantasies such as this ran through my mind continually.

In them, I was never Trygve Soren Napoli. I was always Charles Jones, Bill Tucker, Bob Smith, Jerry Granger, Buddy Thompson.

Inspired by these fantasies, I began to develop a variable personality. Instead of showing a fear-blanked face to the world, I learned how to create a living mask. The living mask was me and not-me. I didn't do it deliberately, nor did it happen overnight. It evolved gradually and was a natural result of what the priest taught us: Retaliate in kind or slink away like a miserable dog. The variable personality allowed you to do both. You could slink away behind a false face without taking one step backwards. You could plan your retaliations behind the face they wanted to see.

ↆ

Mother picked me up at the foster home. "That goddamned Gerald," she said. With those three words she explained and dismissed the entire episode.

I didn't know her very well. In fact, I barely remembered what she looked like. When the train had pulled into Los Angeles's Union Terminal, I realized that I could not identify her in the crowd. Out on the platform a radiant blond stranger looked at me hard. "Trygve?" she said. "Are you my son, Trygve?" I stumbled against her, mute. She pushed me off then shook my hand stiffly. She studied me at arm's length, her North Sea eyes unblinking. "Well, it's been a while," she said. "Three years?" I numbered the years in my head but could not bring myself to correct her. "Four," my grandfather said as he shuffled toward us. "Four damn years." Mother released my hand. "Four is it?" she said. Then, walking away, as if it were up to me to either follow her or not, she added, "Time flies."

She had a way of expressing herself that was similar to her father's. She just said things, and if there was someone nearby to respond, then something like a conversation would ensue. Like my grandfather, she had a Norwegian fatalism, tough enough to outlast winter.

"That goddamned Gerald," she said again. I glanced at her. Her sharp white profile seemed too perfect to be real. I wanted to put my hand on her face, but even the thought of doing such a thing made my heart skip a beat.

Gerald was Gerald Fergus, my uncle. He was in the Canadian navy. His ship had put into Long Beach Harbor to take on supplies which were to be taken to Hawaii. It was December 1942, and the war was exactly one year old. He was on shore leave and had come to visit his sister-in-law and her new husband. His own wife, my mother's sister Ginger, was going to live with us. She was on her way, along with her stepson William, from Vancouver, British Columbia.

"That goddamned Gerald," my mother said a third time. We were in a taxi and once again I was distracted by the passing wonders of the new world. My face pressed against the window, I marveled at the tall palms that lined the streets, common as telephone poles. Exotic flowers on woody vines swept up the sides of small white houses and sometimes covered the houses completely, like glorious camouflage.

My mother released a weary sigh, and I immediately thought of my grandmother. I saw her out at the clothesline with a basket of laundry. The clothes on the line were stretched horizontal to the ground by the constant high-plains gale. My mother's sigh was the breeze of Norwegian resignation. I knew it well. It was sibilant, like the tail end of a curse.

A fatalist believes that nothing can be done, but he will allow himself to be swept along by one cause or another because he believes that being swept along is also something that nothing can be done about. And yet, at least on the surface, she was a fun-lover, festive as a Mexican. Without a second thought she could yell "Hey, where's the party?" to complete strangers from the window of a moving car.

Which is how we got arrested. We had been in Tijuana showing Uncle Gerald a good time. The three of them—my mother, my new stepfather, and Uncle Gerald—went nightclubbing, arm in arm. They left me in the back seat of my stepfather's 1928 Cadillac to wait for them. The kinds of nightclubs they went to would not let in children. I was curious about these nightclubs but too young to be able to imagine what went on inside.

It was a Saturday night and World War II was in full swing somewhere else. Street whores squinted into the Cadillac's windows, checking me out. Their loose, pendulous breasts were rippled by the pulsing neon of Avenida Revolución. Kids younger than me pulled open the doors of the Cadillac and scrambled across the rich mohair upholstery, screaming hilarious Spanish to each other, paying no attention to me at all. I was scared of them, but it was my own fault. I had insisted on coming along to Tijuana. I could have stayed at our apartment in Los Angeles listening to the radio, but I didn't want to be left alone. I didn't want to let my mother out of my sight. She'd been out of sight for four years and I hardly knew her. I knew I couldn't bear to see her drive away in a strange car. An old northern fear would come after me and all the radio programs on the air wouldn't help.

I didn't trust my mother. She was a disappearing woman. I'd seen her come and go years earlier. I had a vague memory of a black car pulling out of my grandparents' driveway. She was in it, with a man. My faulty memory could not put a face on her but I could see a bright red dress printed with flowers, a dark purse, and white high heels. A fragrance moved with her and my longing could not be separated from this fragrance.

I clung to her and whined, risking humiliation. "Take me to Mexico," I sobbed.

"It's your funeral," she said. Norwegian fatalism even applied to children. If I met my fate in Tijuana, what could *she* be expected to do about it?

My stepfather, Mitchell Selfage, was a fast driver. We came back from Tijuana at high speed. The Cadillac roared like a hydroplane racer. The car rose and fell as if it were on water. "This is a *car!*" Mitchell Selfage shouted above the big V-8. He was a car man and had once owned a Hupmobile. Everyone was drunk. I even felt drunk, having inhaled their boozy breaths. My Uncle Gerald was passed out in the back seat. His head was on my lap. He was snoring loud enough to be heard over the engine and road noise. My mother drank beer in the front seat while Mitchell Selfage explained the Cadillac's instrumentation. It was a new car for him. He'd only had it a week.

"Where's the party?" my mother yelled out the window as we roared into Huntington Beach. She yelled it at a car full of laughing people, but managed to attract the notice of a motorcycle cop whom we passed in a blur. Mitchell Selfage was a smooth-talking man with a degree in theater arts from the University of Washington. When the cop pulled us over, Mitchell turned on the charm. He had a wide, engaging smile and the good looks of a leading man. He had just about talked the cop out of giving him a ticket when Uncle Gerald woke up with a loud snort. I saw his eyes pop open wide. His head was still cradled in my lap. The staring head in my lap seemed dangerous to me. I squirmed out from under. Mitchell had just said something that made the cop laugh. Mitchell laughed too. Mitchell's laugh was hair-raising. He laughed on the intake of breath, producing an enormous, rasping sound. If he laughed in public, people from dozens of yards away would stop what they were doing to see what had made the big, inhuman sound. It was a rapturous groan, too monstrous to be produced by ordinary lungs and voice box. It was as if a mythical beast, a minotaur or cyclops, had been dropped into the middle of Los Angeles and had been overcome with hysterics.

It was this alarming sound that made Uncle Gerald's eyes pop open. When he saw the cop leaning into the window, shining a flashlight on Mitchell's driver's license, he muttered a string of black curses. Then he rose up, and in one unbroken motion brought his fist to the policeman's face. It was a solid blow. I heard a tooth crack, a bloody curse, and from my mother, a weary sigh.

↓

Uncle Gerald always got into trouble when he was on shore leave. His full name was Gerald Lawton Fergus. He was from British Columbia and was part Tlingit Indian. He was a fighter and needed almost no provocation, especially when he'd been drinking. Any little thing could set him off. His third wife—my Aunt Ginger—and his son William arrived in Los Angeles the day after Uncle Gerald was let out of jail. He'd had to spend a week there. It was a light sentence but there was a war on and his ship was getting ready to sail.

Mitchell and Uncle Gerald picked Aunt Ginger and William up at the train station and brought them back to our apartment. Whisky vapor came into the apartment with them. They'd stopped for a drink.

"Now then," Uncle Gerald said after we were all seated comfortably in the small living room, "isn't this quite a little family situation?" He bared his teeth and chuckled. Mitchell poured some whisky into Uncle Gerald's glass, and then he poured some into his own. I could tell that he was nervous. Mitchell Selfage was a slender man whose good looks were almost effeminate. Uncle Gerald's tone and manner worried him. Anything could happen when Uncle Gerald had been drinking.

"Maybe you should slack off, Gerald," Aunt Ginger said. "You have to ship out tomorrow morning."

"Chief Petty Officer Ginger," Uncle Gerald said, raising his glass.

"Take it easy, Gerald," my mother said.

Uncle Gerald and Mother exchanged brief glances. My mother was unintimidated. Uncle Gerald looked away first. "What the hell," he said. "It's nearly Christmas." He dug into the pockets of his topcoat. "This is for you, Tryg," he said. He handed me a roll of pennies. "They're brand-new 1943 U.S. pennies. They're zinc, not copper. I got them from the bank."

I took the roll. "Thanks, Uncle Gerald," I said.

"Now, you can waste them on candy machines, but I don't recommend it," he said. He dug another roll of zinc pennies out of his coat and handed them to his son, William. He winked at William. "You know what I'm talking about, don't you, son?"

William was a dark-complected, sullen boy of fifteen. He was tall and thin and his hair was jet black. He hefted the roll of coins, but did not answer his father.

Following William's lead, I began to heft the roll of coins knowledgeably.

"You hit a guy with a roll of these pennies in your fist and he's going to stay hit, Tryg," Uncle Gerald said. "A roll of dimes used to be the ticket, but zinc pennies are better. They're a little lighter than copper pennies but somewhat heavier than dimes."

William and I hefted our zinc pennies.

"A pair of bloody killers," Uncle Gerald said, winking his approval of us.

"How about another drink, Gerald?" Mitchell Selfage said.

"He doesn't need another one," Aunt Ginger said.

Mitchell stopped tilting the bottle toward Uncle Gerald's glass. Uncle Gerald caught the neck of the bottle and forced it down until his glass was filled almost to the brim.

"This is what a woman does," Uncle Gerald said. "She will nettle a man into drinking more than he normally would by her constant bitchiness." He raised his drink to me and winked. "Let this be a lesson to you, Master Trygve. The bitchiness of the female species will cut a man down if he allows it."

He stared at me for a while before he lifted his glass to his lips. I hefted the coins knowledgeably.

Aunt Ginger got up. "Let's all sing Christmas carols," she suggested, smiling as if she really meant it. She walked out.

"You see then what I've been saying, don't you, Trygve?" Uncle Gerald said. "You see my point now, lad?"

I had no choice but to nod gravely and heft the zinc coins.

"How the hell could he see your point, assuming you have one," Mother said. "He's only ten. I don't think you know what you're talking about yourself, Gerald."

Uncle Gerald winked at me again. During all this he focused his attention on me. It made me uncomfortable.

"There it is in a nutshell, Master Trygve," he said. "There's no end to it, lad. Luckily there's this goddamned bloody war. Why do you suppose men love to make war, Trygve? Well, now you know why. It should be as plain as the nose on your face. If it isn't, then you'll have to learn about it the hard way."

"Ask him where he spent the last seven days," my mother said, to no one. "Ask him how much he's learned the easy way."

Uncle Gerald laughed. He drank half his whisky down. Then he drank the other half. "What are we going to do about this?" he said to Mitchell, holding his empty glass up. Mitchell poured whisky into the glass but only filled it up an inch. He poured a small amount into his glass, too.

"Let's coast, Gerald," he said.

William and I went outside, zinc pennies weighting our pockets. We'd been introduced, but so far he hadn't spoken to me. We went to the back of the apartment building where the garbage incinerators were. It was warm, in the seventies. I couldn't get over Los Angeles and its warm climate. Back in Montana it was zero and blowing.

The area between the apartment building and the incinerators was paved. I knelt down and put the flat of my hands against the concrete. "Warm," I said. "Up north it's winter, but it's just like summer here."

"No shit," William said. These were his first words to me. I was startled because his voice was deep, like a man's.

"It's kind of neat," I said.

"I hate this fucking place," he said.

Though he was tall and thin, he looked a lot like his father. His black Indian hair was glossy and combed straight back. He looked like a rugged teenaged Rudolph Valentino from western Canada. His eyes were blue and unblinking.

I couldn't believe he meant that. How could anyone hate Los Angeles? It was the most beautiful place I'd ever seen. Movies and magazines didn't do it justice. Out in front of the apartment building were two fat date palms. They looked like huge pineapples. Their fronds clicked madly in the slightest breeze. I loved that clicking sound. I could hear it from my bedroom at night. To me it was the sound of Los Angeles.

"I guess we're cousins," I said, changing the subject.

"Yeah," he said, "like a turd and a grunt. Guess which one you are."

I left him by the incinerators and walked around the building to the front lawns. I sat under one of the big date palms. Across the street there was an old house. It also had date palms on its front lawn. A girl in shorts was sitting on the porch of the house. Her legs were tanned. She was about twelve or thirteen years old. A car went by. Someone in the car yelled at the girl. She flipped her head back and pretended she didn't hear the boy in the car. She stood up and stretched. Her breasts lifted her blouse, exposing the white skin of her midriff.

I, Charles Jones, held the stick of my crippled Dauntless Dive Bomber and tried to set it down on the carrier. The stick was unresponsive. I was coming in too hard. "Pull up, Charlie," said a voice in my earphones. "Can't, can't," I grunted. I made the roar of the crash and the girl on the porch across the street looked over at me. She made a face and went into her house. Even so, I died a hero in her arms. Her heartbroken tears mixed tragically with the blood on my dead face. "Charlie," she sobbed. "Oh my darling, darling Charlie!"

↓

There were a number of other children in the apartment building, but we were all illegal. The landlord didn't allow children or pets. But there were pets too. I'd seen at least three cats and had heard a small dog bark in a hallway. Whenever the landlord came by, one of the mothers would take out a police whistle and blow it hard. The kids, on hearing this whistle, would get out of the building and run to the vacant lot next to it. There was a dugout "fort" in this vacant lot, big enough to hold the half dozen or so kids who lived in the apartment building. We'd all cram into our underground fort and wait for the "All Clear," which was three short blasts from a whistle. It was great fun, like war itself.

Uncle Gerald continued drinking that day. He went out alone and came back late at night, very drunk. He'd been fighting. His lips were caked with blood and his left eye was swollen shut. It was 3 A.M. William and I had been asleep for a while. We were sharing the same bed. There weren't enough rooms in the apartment for him to have his own bedroom. A loud string of horrible curses woke us up. We got out of bed and peeked into the hallway. Uncle Gerald was yelling at Aunt Ginger. She had her hands up to her ears and she was crying. "Don't lie about it," Uncle Gerald said. "I know what the hell you've been up to. I'm on to your tricks. Do you take me for a bloody moron?"

Then he hit her. I saw him do it. So did William. It was so shocking to see a grown man punch a grown woman in the face that I almost fainted. Aunt Ginger fell down on her back. She rolled over against the wall, and, to protect herself from further punishment, curled up into a tight ball.

"Christ," William said, in disgust.

Uncle Gerald saw us then. He came after us. We scrambled back into the bedroom and made for the window. It was a ground-level apartment and we went out into the grassy stubble that bordered the building. Then we sprinted away, to the vacant lot, and into the fort. Uncle Gerald didn't follow us.

There was no sound in the dark fort other than our heavy breathing. We sat there for several minutes, listening to our lungs empty and fill. We were in our pajamas, shivering.

"I'm going to join the American marines," William said.

"You can't," I said. "You've got to be at least seventeen."

"I look seventeen," he said. "You can get a fake birth certificate in Tijuana."

What did he know of Tijuana? He was from Canada, a thousand miles north. "I've been there," I said, casually.

"Did you get a dose?" he said.

I didn't know what he meant. I knew that 'dos' was Mexican for 'two.' So, 'a dos' must mean a pair. Did I get a pair. I still didn't know what he was talking about.

After a minute he laughed. "Where've you been all your life?" he asked.

"Mostly in Montana," I said.

"That figures."

We went back to the apartment the same way we left it, through the window. It was nearly four in the morning. I was hungry and thirsty. I went into the hallway and tiptoed toward the kitchen. The kitchen was on the other side of the living room. The Murphy bed in the living room was pulled down. There was someone in it. There was a lot of movement and gasping.

"I'm so sorry my darling Ginger," Uncle Gerald said. "Oh, my darling Ginger, I am so sorry."

"I know, I know," Aunt Ginger said softly.

I finished tiptoeing into the kitchen, got a glass of milk and some saltines, and tiptoed back into my own bedroom. After I had my milk and crackers I lay in bed thinking. I thought about my Uncle Gerald and my Aunt Ginger. He'd tried to hurt her, but now he was kissing her and asking for forgiveness, which she was willing to give. Aunt Ginger was a beautiful woman who liked to read novels. She always had a dreamy look in her eyes, as if something that happened long ago and far away occupied her thoughts. "Long Ago and Far Away" was her favorite song. She had the record and played it a lot on our RCA Victrola. She was twenty-five years old, four years younger than my mother. She was quiet and romantic and I was half in love with her. I often saw her stranded in Germany, waiting for rescue. I, special agent Charles Jones, would parachute into Germany with a tommy gun and shortwave radio. We'd work our way across the mountains and into Switzerland, listening to "Long Ago and Far Away" on the shortwave.

"There's something you've got to know," William said, breaking into my dream world.

"What," I said.

"I'm serious."

"*What?*" I repeated.

"I'm clearing out. I'm not going to go to that stupid high school. I can't stand it here."

"So you're going back to Canada."

"What?"

"Back to Canada. You're going there."

"Jesus. Can't you pay attention? I said I was going to join the marines."

I didn't believe him, but I didn't want to get into an argument. "So, when are you going?" I said. "Tomorrow?"

"I'll go when the time is right."

"The war will probably be over next year," I said.

"Bull," he said.

"I hope it lasts until 1950," I said. "I'll be old enough then to join the Army Air Corps' pilot school."

William barked out a single scornful laugh. "You're not the hero type, kid," he said.

I resented this. Here I'd had to share my bedroom and bed with him and now he was insulting me. "I could do it if I had to," I said.

He laughed rudely again. "You ever been in a fight? A real fight?"

I thought about that. "Yes," I said.

"I bet. Did you pound the crap out of someone?" He was enjoying himself immensely at my expense.

"Sure," I said.

"Who? Tell me his name and tell me why and where you had to fight him." He put his tongue in his cheek. He winked.

"Sylvester Snell," I said. "At the foster home. He bothered some of the littler kids. I told him to quit. He wouldn't quit so I pounded on him. He was older than me, around your age."

In my mind I watched myself knock Sylvester Snell down. I saw him roll away from me and curl up in a protective ball. "Don't hit me again," he pleaded. I had the zinc pennies in my fist.

William laughed again. Then he farted. "Gone with the wind," he said.

↓

Christmas came and went. I got a two-tube shortwave radio kit and William got a Daisy B B gun. My mother was hired by the Douglas Aircraft Company as a riveter. She riveted the aluminum skins of Dauntless Dive Bombers to their frames. Aunt Ginger was hired by Douglas shortly after Mother was. She was a "bucker," the person opposite the riveter who held up a metal plate against the rivet so that it would flatten out as it came through the skin. Buckers made less than riveters, but even at that the pay was good. There was a lot of money coming into the household. Mitchell Selfage made the most money, though, because he was involved in the black market. He was a milkman and was able to trade butter, cream, and cheese for gasoline stamps which he sold at several times their value. The rationing of gasoline had put a serious crimp in the freedom to travel, and in Los Angeles, the freedom to travel by automobile was more precious than any freedom guaranteed by the Constitution. Without the ability to drive wherever and whenever they wanted to, the people of Los Angeles suffered emotional disturbance. They felt their lives were drab without the free use of their cars, even though, at that time, Los Angeles had one of the best public transit systems in the country. Electric trains criss-crossed the county, and for a ten-cent token you could go almost anywhere. William and I often took an electric train to Santa Monica or Venice from our west-side apartment building.

During the dead days after Christmas and before the start of the new school term, William and I spent a lot of our time together. Unlike most teenagers, he was not ashamed to be seen hanging around with a ten-year-old kid. He was not intimidated by what other people thought of him. In fact, he had a natural, good-natured belligerence that dared anyone to criticize his behavior. I wanted to blend in, to be part of the well-behaved crowd, to present the face others expected to see. But William was always himself and challenged anyone, by his demeanor and sharp glances, to find fault. Whenever we were together, I felt endangered. William was a magnet for trouble.

Once, when we were washing and polishing Mitchell Selfage's Cadillac, William said, "You want to go for a spin?" He had found where Mitchell kept the keys and he waved them in the air in front of my eyes.

I thought he was kidding, so I said, "Sure thing."

William got behind the wheel and switched on the ignition. "Get in," he said.

I got in, still thinking he didn't have the nerve to really do it. Mitchell was at work and wouldn't be home for several hours. Even so, I didn't think William knew how to drive a car.

I was wrong. He stepped on the starter and the big eight roared alive. He depressed the clutch and moved the long gear lever into reverse. We backed out of Mitchell's designated parking slot behind the apartment, and into the alley that ran along behind it. Then he shifted into first and the car moaned forward.

"Wait up," I said, "you'd better stop here."

William laughed and stepped on the gas. The alley was heavily graveled and a spray of small stones spewed into the air behind us.

"See if you can get something on the radio," he said.

The radio was as old as the car—there were too many knobs and dials. I managed eventually to switch it on and find a station. The Merry Macs were singing "Mairzy Doats." The jumpy little tune made William feed the big engine more gas and we hit the street at rubber-burning speed.

William circled around to the street that our apartment building fronted. I saw the girl who lived across from us sunning her legs. She saw me but if she recognized me she didn't show it.

I was Lieutenant Bill Tucker, taking off in my B-17. I wasn't sure the runway was long enough since we were carrying an extra heavy load of bombs. This time we were going to level Berlin. "This could be it," I said into my microphone. The suntanned girl in the control tower began to cry.

"This could be what?" William said.

"Huh? I just meant we could get into trouble."

William raised up off the seat a little and farted. "Gone with the wind," he said.

We circled the block several times. Lieutenant Tucker leveled Berlin but was badly shot up. The tail section of the B-17 looked like Swiss cheese. Lieutenant Tucker noticed that blood was seeping through his sheep-lined flight jacket. "Bail out, men," he said. "I'll keep it level as long as I can." His co-pilot said, "What about you, Bill?" Lieutenant Tucker smiled sadly. "I've had it, Charlie. Forget about me. Just tell…Elizabeth that I…" I didn't know what Lieutenant Tucker would have said to Elizabeth, so I just let him die quietly in the smoking ruins of the B-17.

"What the hell are you whispering about?" William asked.

I thought I'd been more careful but I'd allowed my lips to move and some air to escape. "Nothing," I said sullenly.

When William reparked the Cadillac, I rewashed the big, wood-spoked wheels to erase any evidence of our illicit travels.

One night, William and I went to the movies. The closest theater, the Variety, was showing the horror movie *The Isle of the Dead,* starring Boris Karloff. The tanned girl from across the street was there by herself. William sat next to her and I sat next to William. Sometime during the movie I noticed that William had his arm resting on the back of the tanned girl's seat, and soon after that, directly on her shoulders. They didn't speak to each other or in any way acknowledge each other's existence. After the movie, when we were walking home, William said, "The tits are real."

But my mind had been thrown into a mood of morbid speculation by the frightening movie and I could not fully register what he said.

↓

The dream started off fine. Most nightmares do. I was a baby again, with the New York Italians. My mother was nowhere in sight. It was a festive occasion. I was being bounced from lap to lap as my uncles played guitars and accordians. The rich perfume of spaghetti sauce saturated the tenement. Guido, the uncle no one ever talked about, danced happily around the groaning table. He stomped on the linoleum until the dishes fell from the cupboards. My father took me in his arms and whirled me around over his head. But then he wasn't my father, he was my Norwegian grandfather and suddenly it wasn't fun anymore. The music stopped and all I could hear was the northern wind as it banged against the house like a madman enraged by rejection. The door flew open and the madman was my grandfather who now looked like Boris Karloff, and I knew that I was on the Isle of the Dead, trapped. The coffin I was to be buried alive in was being assembled in the kitchen. I screamed, waking myself.

I got to the bathroom just in time. My nervous kidneys had filled my bladder. I said a prayer of thanks that I hadn't wet the bed. How could I have explained it to William?

I was afraid to get back into bed—the dream might not be done with me. I sat down at the little table in the corner of the bedroom and switched on my two-tube shortwave receiver, which I had recently finished building. I put the headset on, plugged in a coil for the forty-nine-meter band, and began sweeping the dial around for stations. I picked up Mexico or South America, then New Zealand. I couldn't believe it! New Zealand! I wanted to wake William up but he was a heavy sleeper and hated to be disturbed. I woke him up once because a squadron of heavy bombers was flying over the apartment building and you could see what seemed like a thousand flashing lights in the sky. But William came out of the bed with his fists clenched, his eyes frighteningly wide.

New Zealand faded and I tuned in to something that sounded like Japanese. It seemed to be conversation in quick bursts, and I imagined Japanese bombers moving toward some innocent target in the dead of night. I gave myself over to this fantasy, becoming Lieutenant Jerry Granger, P-38 pilot. Our squadron was scrambled from our Pacific Atoll base and we climbed quickly to meet the enemy. Mitsubishi Zeroes dropped out of the sun, killing Lieutenant Bob Smith, my wingman. Bob went down in brilliant flames. The Army Air Corps anthem played slow as a dirge as Bob's "Lightning" exploded into the sea. But vengeance was mine. I climbed above the Zeroes and came down on them, all four .50-caliber machine guns blazing, along with the twenty-millimeter cannon. The Zeroes disintegrated in the air before my eyes. It was a total victory, won in less than a minute, but it was tinged with tragedy. I'd lost my best friend. The Air Corps anthem was heavy in the air as I did my victory roll.

"Shut up, will you?" William said. He'd pulled a pillow over his head. I guess I was humming the Air Corps anthem out loud. I took off the headset and switched off my receiver.

The next morning was Saturday. We all had breakfast together—Mitchell Selfage, Aunt Ginger, Mother, William, and I. It was flapjacks and fried Spam, my favorite. William and I took turns doing the dishes and today was my day to do them, but Mitchell Selfage stopped me after I'd cleared the table. "I'd like to discuss a matter of considerable importance with you, Trygve," he said.

Mitchell Selfage looked something like the actor Zachary Scott. He had elegant ways and always used proper English. He wanted to get into the movies. He already knew how to act, having majored in it at the University of Washington. His job as a milkman, he said, was a temporary thing. As soon as he got his break, he'd quit. He knew he looked a lot like Zachary Scott and cultivated the similarity. For instance, he grew a thin mustache just like Zachary Scott's. He oiled his hair and combed it straight back, like the actor's. Zachary Scott always played the role of a slightly felonious manipulator. He usually wound up getting shot or being thrown down a flight of stairs by some more American-looking actor such as John Garfield or Alan Ladd. He was charming to a certain kind of vulnerable woman. But all his charm was in his slick talk and cheap good looks. Even though you'd see him in a black-and-white movie, you could *smell* him. The smell was of a sickly cologne that made you gag.

Mitchell Selfage was like that. Thin, good-looking, with a tight, well-trimmed mustache winging his upper lip. He had a deformity, though, which saved him from being completely like Zachary Scott. He had a small knob of flesh in the middle of his forehead, just under the hairline. It was hard to keep your eyes away from it when you had to speak to him. You could see him get mad as he became aware of the fact that people were not looking into his eyes but at the unusual knob of flesh on his forehead. It undercut the seriousness of what he was saying to them.

The knob made me think there was a horn under it trying to sprout. Any day now it would split and a white bone tip would begin to project from it. How could I take my eyes from it when he spoke to me? It was the most interesting thing about him.

We sat at opposite ends of the table. Mother and Aunt Ginger went out for a walk. William was in the front room, listening to the radio. I folded my hands on the table in front of me and looked at them. Two long hairs grew out of the back of my right hand. They were dark and coarse. What did that mean? Was I turning into an ape?

"May I have your attention, Trygve?" Mitchell said.

"Sure," I said.

"Not 'sure,' Trygve," he said. "You say, 'Yes, sir, you may.'"

I didn't know what to say. The hairs were awful looking. Why hadn't I seen them before? Had they grown there overnight?

"Look at me, Trygve," Mitchell said.

I looked at him, or rather, at the knob of flesh on his forehead.

"You have some obscene habits, Trygve," he said.

"I know," I said, confessing cooperatively, even though I wasn't sure what "obscene" meant. I knew it wasn't a compliment, and that it had something to do with disgust. I looked at my ape hands again. I felt depressed and hungry again for fried Spam and flapjacks.

"You *know*, do you?" he said. He was smiling and sneering. I thought of Zachary Scott bilking Joan Crawford for everything she was worth because she was too blinded by his sleazy good looks to know better.

He didn't say anything for a while. It made me nervous. I racked my brains, trying to think of the obscene things I had done.

"It's the way I eat," I said. I was thinking of how I loved to heap peas up against mashed potatoes with my fork, spearing the uncooperative ones as if they were Japs. Or of my way of scraping gravy across my plate so that it would pool up on one side, then dipping bread into it. Or maybe it was the way I would take a slice of Spam and put it between two flapjacks to make a kind of sandwich.

"No," he said, "not the way you eat, though there is much in the way of improvement that can be made in that area."

His knob glowed like a miner's lamp as the sunlight from the kitchen window caught it.

"I'm talking about the way you walk, Trygve," he said.

"The way I walk?"

"Do I hear an echo? Yes, Trygve, the way you *walk*."

I was astonished. There was no "way" to walk. You just did it. You walked. You ran. Or you stood still.

"You walk like a clodhopper. Is that the way the Swedes, or Norwegians, or whatever they are, walk in Montana?"

"Well, yes," I said, again in the spirit of cooperation. I wanted to freely admit my guilt, but I also wanted to let the Norwegians and Swedes of Montana take the brunt of the blame. If I walked like a clodhopper, it was their fault because that's how *they* walked. Californians, I reasoned, shouldn't have to put up with clodhopper ways of walking. It made perfect sense to me.

"Of course I don't *blame* you, Trygve. You can't be held responsible for poor training."

I felt a surge of gratitude. I walked like a clodhopper, but it wasn't my fault. Just like the knob of flesh on Mitchell's forehead wasn't *his* fault. It was just there, a fact of life.

"Luckily, something can be done about it, Trygve. I'm going

to teach you the proper way to walk." He stood up suddenly. "Watch me," he said.

He walked in slow motion across the kitchen. I had noticed before this that he was a very graceful man, but I never pinpointed the reasons why I thought so. Clearly, it was in the way he moved. He walked in a gliding way, like an ice skater. It was smooth, almost like dancing.

"Now, you try it, Trygve," he said.

I panicked. I didn't know what to do to get that gliding motion into my walk. I tiptoed across the floor.

Mitchell laughed. It was his big groaning laugh coming on the intake of breath. "Oh, Lord," he said. "You look like you're sneaking into a peep show. Watch me again, Trygve."

I watched his feet carefully. He walked like a cat—quietly and with no bounce. But I didn't see how he was doing it.

"Now, try it again, Trygve," he said.

I pretended I was in Montana, ice-skating on a pond. I moved like a skater, sliding along the linoleum.

"Excellent!" he said, clapping his hands together hard. "Very close, Trygve. The only trouble is you don't look very natural. You look pained. Walking properly is not painful."

He walked around the kitchen in slow motion. I followed him, cutting a smooth track in the ice, my hands folded behind my back.

"You see it now, don't you, Trygve?" he said.

"I think so," I said. "You don't let your heels come down. You stay on your toes."

"Not toes, Trygve. I stay on the balls of my feet, balanced."

We went around the room again, smooth as skaters.

"Balls first, balls first," he chanted as we slid around the kitchen. "Allow the heels to touch, but do not let your weight fall on them completely. Let your balls do the main job, always the balls."

He sat down and motioned for me to continue walking. He wanted to observe me do it. "Beyond esthetic advantages," he said, "it's excellent exercise. You'll have superb calves if you learn to walk properly." He pulled up his pantleg and flexed his white calf. It was dainty and muscular at the same time.

My own calves were aching from the exercise.

"You'll thank me one day for this lesson in proper walking, Trygve," he said.

I sat down again, opposite him. We were both breathing heavily from all the exercise. I noticed a third hair, smaller than the other two but just as coarse, growing on the back of my hand. *Werewolf,* I thought, watching, in my mind, Lon Chaney, Jr., running like a clodhopper through the woods as his skin became furry, barking and howling in spite of himself.

"This won't mean anything to you now, Trygve," Mitchell said, "but one day you'll find that most women do not like to see shapeless calves on a man."

I looked up at him then because I felt he expected me to. I couldn't meet his eyes. I looked at the knob on his forehead. I imagined it bursting, a long shaft of white bone rising out of it, a hard twisted cone, like the horn of a unicorn.

↓

Aunt Ginger was a little crazy. I didn't realize it at the time since I accepted all behavior, except my own, as normal. I often overheard my mother scolding her. "You can't do that," my mother said once. "I won't let you do it."

I didn't know what she was talking about but from the tone of her voice, I knew it was something serious. One afternoon, when I was alone in the apartment, Aunt Ginger came in. There was a man with her. "Don't tell on me, Tryg," she said. She had a sad little smile on her lips, but her eyes were distant and unconcerned.

The man was in uniform, an army corporal. He gave me two new dimes. "Why don't you run out to the store and buy yourself some geedunks," he said. He winked at me. By "geedunks" he meant candy. I'd heard other soldiers use that word on the train coming to Los Angeles.

I got my jacket and went out. In the hallway, I heard "Long Ago and Far Away" coming from our Victrola.

Once Aunt Ginger said to me, "I have lived many lives, Trygve."

She was sitting on the bed in my bedroom while I tuned my shortwave receiver. She bounced up and down, like a kid. I thought of her as kind of a kid, but I'd realize later that her childlike ways were really a manifestation of her madness.

"No, really," she said, even though I didn't object. I wouldn't have known what I was objecting to, anyway. "I was once a little Russian princess. And before that, I was a knight of the realm. I mean it! A knight in shining armor. I fought against the Saracens."

In my earphones I heard a man with an English accent say, "We have suffered greatly, we shall suffer more, but we shall prevail."

"So you see how relative it all is," she said.

"I guess so," I said.

"I mean, this war and everything. For someone in the distant future, it will be a thing of the past, like a dream."

"Uh-huh," I said.

"As far as I'm concerned, it's *already* a dream."

I tuned away from the English-accented man and found some pleasant-sounding Morse code.

"I'm serious. I feel as though everything that's going on now is a dream, like I could wake up from it into another type of world completely, or I could fall into deeper sleep and it would all disappear. That would be best, I think. To go under completely until it was gone, all of it, gone."

She began to cry. She lay down on my bed and curled up into a ball and sobbed. She looked like she'd been punched.

The flurry of dots and dashes in my earphones seemed like a desperate message that needed an immediate reply, but I couldn't understand it.

↙

That night I dreamed about Sylvester Snell. I dreamed Aunt Ginger and I had been talking in the kitchen when someone blew the police whistle warning the kids to clear out of the building. We all ran out. Aunt Ginger ran along beside me. I didn't think it was unusual at all for her to be running with us. But then I couldn't find the fort. He was behind us, the landlord, making an awful noise. When I turned to look at him, it was Sylvester, fanged and horned, his eyes dead serious gray. I froze. But he didn't come after me. Instead, he went after Aunt Ginger. He caught her by the hair and then socked her. She fell down hard. They were out in the empty lot and I was still frozen in my tracks by the apartment building. Then Sylvester began to drag her under. Under the ground. They both disappeared into a hole in the ground. The lot was empty again.

Sylvester was the devil. I understood that now and the realization unfroze me. I ran out to the middle of the lot, screaming a prayer at the top of my lungs, willing myself to become Charlie Jones, Bill Tucker, Buddy Thompson—any true hero, indifferent to danger, untouched by fear.

↙

"What kind of a name is Trygve Napoli?" the teacher asked. It was my first day in class at the Marvin Street School. I was in 4-B, a second-semester fourth-grader.

"Italian," I mumbled, my face hot.

The teacher's name was Miss Porter. She was tall and very narrow, like a stick figure. "Well, *perhaps*," she said, smiling impersonally. "Perhaps *Napoli* is Italian, but I don't think *Trygve* is. Tell us all about yourself, Trygve. Tell us about your name and where you came from. I think the other children would be very interested."

It was a horrible moment. The other children were staring at me. I felt they had already decided that I could not be one of them. Smirks, sneers, and blank stares. I began to panic. I couldn't think of anything to say.

"Come on, Trygve," Miss Porter said. "Don't be bashful."

"I, uh. I, uh," I said, and the children snickered.

"Courtesy! Courtesy, children!" Miss Porter said. "Speak louder, Trygve. In fact, I want you to come up here, by my desk."

I staggered down the aisle toward her. Fingers tugged at my pants. A girl bent down to tie her shoelace, blocking my way. I tried to sidestep her but her head bumped my thigh. When she let me pass, she made a face as if at a strong odor.

"Now then," Miss Porter said when I reached her desk. "Turn around and face the class and tell them all about where you came from."

I faced them. My throat tightened. The girl who had blocked the aisle was rolling her eyes dramatically, as if to say, Who *cares* where he came from?

"Montana," I said.

"Montana," said Miss Porter. "Well, what *about* Montana? Is it another planet? Is it in South America? Is it a street? I believe there is a street in Santa Monica called Montana Street."

The children, who had been suppressing their laughter, now understood that it was all right to laugh out loud, and they did.

"Courtesy! Courtesy!" Miss Porter shouted, tapping her desk with her pointer. "Now, Trygve, tell us where, exactly, Montana is."

She pulled a map of the United States down out of a cylindrical map case. She handed me the pointer. I stepped around her desk and pointed at Montana.

"My, that's an awfully large state," Miss Porter said. "Can you show us more precisely what part of it you came from?"

I ran the tip of the pointer around in a little circle somewhere in the north-central part of Montana.

"Excellent," Miss Porter said. "Now, Trygve, do you realize that some of the children here have never seen *snow*?"

I looked at them, my self-consciousness momentarily gone. Was it possible? How could anyone not have seen snow? I looked at the mocking faces. Some of them were ignorant of snow!

"Tell us about snow, Trygve," Miss Porter said. "Tell us about blizzards."

The problem of describing a snowstorm to someone who had never seen snow stumped me. "Well, it gets real cold," I said. "Then the wind blows hard. Then it snows."

"Interesting, Trygve, but not very descriptive," said Miss Porter. "Could you tell us more, such as some of your personal experiences with snow and cold weather?"

"I found a dead cat in the woodpile once," I said. "It was frozen solid. I told my grandpa and when he pulled it out its tail broke off."

The children shrieked with laughter. Miss Porter slapped her desk over and over with a yardstick as if she were beating a stubborn animal. "Oh, that's *grotesque*, Trygve!" she said after the class had calmed down. "And I know you made that up, young man! I have a cat, Pierre. He's *very* intelligent. Pierre would not allow himself to be frozen. He would make a nest for himself, in a sheltered place."

"It was trying to make a nest for itself," I said. "But it didn't matter. When it gets fifty below and the wind blows hard, a cat will freeze, even Pierre."

Miss Porter didn't argue with children. She smiled sadly and rolled the map back into its case. "You have a vivid imagination, young Mister Napoli"—this made the children laugh again, and whether Miss Porter meant to or not, she had dubbed me with a nickname: Young Mister Napoli—"but a vivid imagination is no substitute for a clearly stated fact, is it children?"

In a single delighted voice that sounded like the scream of a triumphant nightmare creature, the children shouted, "*NO!*"

↓

I developed a strange affliction that year. I couldn't think without moving my lips. I whispered all my thoughts, including the most shameful ones. Even if I spoke my mind aloud, I'd find myself repeating the words again, just under my breath, in a soft whisper. It was as if I had an intimate but slow-witted companion who needed to have everything I said or thought repeated privately into his ear. It was embarrassing.

I'd lost the ability to keep things to myself.

Mitchell Selfage was the first to notice my problem. He'd been greatly pleased with my improved walking style, but now he was disappointed in me again.

"You're repeating yourself, Trygve," he said.

We were in his milk truck. Sometimes on Saturdays he liked me to ride along with him, to help with the heavier deliveries. He paid me half a dollar. His route took him into Hollywood, which was not very far from where we lived. We would drive up Pico Boulevard, turn north on La Cienega, then left on Melrose. He liked to stop at Don the Beachcomber's over on McCadden Place for lunch. Some of the lesser-known movie actors ate there and Mitchell wanted to get to know them. "You don't start at the top," he once said. "That's a typical beginner's mistake. You make contacts at the low end of the totem pole, then you work your way upstairs."

It was after we'd had roast beef on rye at Don the Beachcomber's that he caught me whispering something I'd just said out loud.

"I think I saw Bob Steele," I said, repeating it seconds later to my invisible, slow-witted companion.

"I heard you the first time," Mitchell said.

"Maybe it was someone else, though," I said. "Maybe it was someone else, though," I whispered.

"You did it again," he said.

"I know," I said. "I know," I whispered.

"It's very annoying, Trygve. Try to stop it, will you? It's a very foolish habit."

"I'll try," I said. I turned my face from him and repeated myself, cupping my mouth in my hand as if I were about to cough.

We drove up into a nice residential district in the hills. "That's where Franchot Tone lives," he said.

I'd just seen a great Franchot Tone movie and so I immediately perked up. It was a war movie, tanks in North Africa. It was realistic. I believed that's how it was in North Africa—tanks droning through heavy sand, laboring up and down dunes, the men sunburned and half crazy with thirst.

Mitchell parked the truck and set the brake. "We'll just hang around a while," he said. "Maybe Mr. Tone will drop in. You never know." We were in front of a large white house.

Mitchell gave me a half-pint bottle of chocolate milk for a mid-afternoon snack. He opened a quart of buttermilk for himself. We sat drinking milk from glass bottles in front of Franchot Tone's house in Hollywood, California, U.S.A., just as if it were the most normal thing in the world. My excitement made me drink my milk in short, quick sips.

After about a half hour, Mitchell started up the truck and we finished the route.

On the way home I said, "Are you going into the army, Mitchell?" I whispered it again into my hand.

His face went white. He reached over and grabbed the front of my shirt, jerking me forward on the seat. "Don't ever mention army to me, Trygve," he said. "It's very bad luck. The draft is breathing down my neck. So far I've been lucky. But if you start blabbing out loud about it my luck might be spoiled." He let me go and calmed himself down a bit. "I'd go, of course, if called," he said. "It's just that I don't have time for the army. I'm trying to start a career."

"Career?" I said. "Career?" I whispered.

"Films," he said. "The cinema. Do you think I *want* to deliver milk for a living? It's a dead-end job, Trygve. It's rent money and food on the table plus a few extras, but that's *it*."

I would have given anything to fly P-38s, and yet Mitchell Selfage, who could have flown them if he wanted to, preferred civilian life.

Once he thought he saw Franchot Tone peeking out at us through the drapes. We'd been parked in front of his house for over half an hour. Mitchell straightened his bow tie, and hopped out of the truck. He opened the side of the truck and began to rearrange milk cases, taking bottles from near-empty cases and loading them into cases that were only partially empty. A man came out of the house. He stepped off the front steps and stared at us. "What do you think you're doing?" he asked.

Mitchell, a case of empties rattling in his hands, said, "Well, Mr. *Tone!* What an extraordinary pleasure this is!"

"Your milk is going to get sour if you don't move that truck out of the sun. Are you planning to spend the whole goddamned day parked in front of my house?"

If it was Franchot Tone, he didn't sound anything like he did in *Five Graves to Cairo.*

"No, sir!" Mitchell said. "Just taking a break. I'm terribly sorry for the inconvenience, Mr. Tone."

Mitchell looked crestfallen. He pulled his milkman's cap down on his forehead so that the lump at the hairline was hidden.

"You got any buttermilk on that rig?" Franchot Tone said.

Mitchell perked up instantly. He gave Franchot Tone his best, lady-killing smile. "Oh, yes indeed, Mr. Tone!" he said. "I've got good, fresh buttermilk in both quarts and pints."

"Sell me a pint, will you? I've got a board in my head and a stomach full of pissed-off scorpions."

"No, sir," Mitchell said. "I won't *sell* you any buttermilk. It's on the house, compliments of Mitchell Selfage."

Franchot Tone looked at Mitchell as if Mitchell's dazzling smile was giving him a worse headache than he already had. "Thanks, Mitch," he said, accepting the pint of buttermilk. He drank it down, handed Mitchell the empty, then walked back into his house.

"I don't think that was Franchot Tone," I said as we drove back to the Challenge Milk Company warehouse. I bit my tongue but I could feel it flexing with the words it needed to repeat.

"You don't know what you're talking about," Mitchell said.

"I think Franchot Tone has more hair on his head," I said. I started to whisper it again, but Mitchell pinched my cheek, stopping me.

"You've seen one Franchot Tone movie and suddenly you're an expert," he said, nastily.

"Two," I said. "Two," I whispered.

"That doesn't mean a thing. No movie star looks the same in real life. You've got to take into consideration the makeup, the natural distortions of the camera lens. Many things do not translate well from real life and vice versa."

He was over my head, so I didn't try to argue with him. I just remembered Franchot Tone, sitting in an Algiers bar, looking hard and lean and war weary. The man Mitchell gave free buttermilk to was nearly bald, had a lumpish pot belly, and was wearing green denim work clothes. He didn't look fit for war.

"Franchot Tone," Mitchell said dreamily. "Jesus, Franchot Tone himself."

↓

Azad Yaznur was new to the Marvin Street School. He arrived a week after me. He came from some Near Eastern country and his English was not very good. Better still, he was fat. This made him a more likely subject for ridicule than me.

Azad was singled out quickly. "German spy! German spy!" the children would shout, chasing the fat boy around the playground. There was nothing German about Azad, but that didn't matter. He was alien, different, and that was enough. He qualified as a German spy on those grounds alone.

I was ecstatic. I'd had enough of "Young Mister Napoli." Girls on the swings would ride high into the air chanting "Young Mister

Napoli" as loud as they could in clear, bell-like voices. I'd made the mistake, shortly after the school term began, of falling in love. The girl, Jane Webster, was a crisp blond in pigtails. She sat at the desk behind me. I couldn't get her out of my mind. At night I'd visualize her on the bedroom ceiling, swinging high in the Marvin Street School playground. To prove my love, I showed her a way to encode secret messages. I'd learned how to do it from a Captain Marvel comic book. You'd write the alphabet down, then write it again, backwards, directly under the first alphabet. Then you'd match the letters of the word you wanted to encode with the letters from the second alphabet. So "I Like You" would come out "R Orpv Blf." Jane seemed interested while I was showing her this ingenious coding principle, but out on the playground during recess, she and her friends gave me funny looks. They ran from me, giggling, and I heard the dreaded chant, "Young Mister NAH-poly," over and over. So when Azad Yaznur came along and was singled out as our German spy, I was so relieved that I joined his tormentors.

Every recess we'd chase Azad and call him spy. He didn't understand what was going on, and was frightened. He was short and very soft-looking. He had a silky black mustache—Near Eastern peach fuzz—and smooth olive skin. He was always dressed nicely, in slacks, shined shoes, and a clean, long-sleeved shirt buttoned to the neck. When he ran from us, we'd pursue him, chanting.

I won the approval of the other children by inventing a harrowing chant designed to terrorize German spies:

> German spy! German spy!
> Adolf Hitler
> Is going to DIE!

Azad would cover his ears and run, but we were relentless.

My enthusiastic persecution of Azad Yaznur was all the more energetic since it was a celebration of my acceptance by the other children. Once, when the other children had found something more interesting to do, I found myself chasing Azad alone. I cornered him by a backstop.

> German spy! German spy!
> Adolf Hitler
> Is going to DIE!

I bullied him into a corner. He began to cry. His sobs were enormous, whining moans that gave voice to the injustice of his situation. He was in agony, but I didn't feel good about it because no one else was *there*. Persecution required a mob. It was a communal effort. Without a mob it became personal. It became me against Azad, and I had nothing against Azad personally. Our confrontation became a mute juxtaposition of unformed selves. Azad stopped crying. I stopped chanting. I didn't know what to say. I said, "Spy." I said it gently. "Spy," I whispered.

Azad hit my nose with his soft fist. "Yon Meester NAW-poly," he said.

Tears rushed out of my eyes. The trickle on my lip, I was astonished to see, was red. Azad ran away chanting, "Yon Meester NAW-poly," while I stood next to the backstop, bleeding. I felt intense embarrassment, thankful that no one had noticed the incident. I stayed by the backstop until my nose stopped trickling.

Azad and I became friends. We sensed each other's more or less irrevocable status as outsiders. It was a negative bond; we didn't especially like each other. But I often went to his house after school. The Yaznur house was an old bungalow on Marvin Street. His mother kept it dark inside. It seemed mysterious to me, full of strange smells and stranger music. Azad's room had a tapestry on the wall. He had a low bed, blanketed with richly embroidered covers. He had no toys, but he had a big Philco table model radio with four shortwave bands on it. We spent many afternoons listening tirelessly to the excited voices of the wartime world. Then, when it was time for our programs, we switched to the broadcast band for Hop Harrigan, Terry and the Pirates, Superman, and Captain Midnight.

I continued to love Jane Webster, though I barely spoke to her now. She and her friends still gave me odd, eye-rolling looks when I walked past them. I wrote her a rhyming love note in code.

R GSRMP BLFIV KIVGGB
R GSRMP BLFIV MRXV
RU BLF DVIV Z PRGGB
RW UVVW BLF NRXV

(I think you're pretty/I think you're nice/If you were a kitty/I'd feed you mice.) It was pretty stupid, and I knew it. I never gave it to her. So I was astonished and then thrilled when Jane gave *me* a note in our code:

BLF HNVOO ORPV KVV
GZPV Z YZGS

She slipped it into my hand after school. My heart skipped a beat. She seemed more beautiful than ever. Her eyes made my knees feel weak. They were large, pale blue eyes that always looked shocked. The white around the blue was starkly prominent. It was as if she had seen something incredible—like explosions on the moon. And though the sight delighted her, there was also an annoyed look in her eyes when she looked at you—you were so much *less* than a lunar explosion.

I didn't stop at Azad's that afternoon, even though he tugged at my sweater sleeve until it was stretched several inches too long for my arm. I had to punch him on the shoulder a dozen times to get him to let go. Then I ran all the way back to our apartment building.

I scribbled the alphabet, then scribbled it again in reverse. I decoded the love note carefully, wanting to dwell on each letter, not wanting the deciphering process to end. I could have spent the rest of my life working out love's wonderful cryptology.

The message was blunt and horrifying:

YOU SMELL LIKE PEE
TAKE A BATH

I took off my blue jeans and smelled the crotch. Pee. The dank pee smell almost burned my eyes. I vowed to change my jeans and shorts at least twice a week from then on. But as far as Jane Webster was concerned, we were finished. Those amazed eyes never looked at me again.

↓

William and I took the Pacific Electric train to Santa Monica. It was a Saturday morning and the Big Red Car was packed with beachgoers. Even though it was February, the Santa Ana wind was blowing—red wind, some people called it—bringing in warm air from the desert. By 10 A.M., the temperature was in the high seventies. By late afternoon it was supposed to be in the nineties. I was looking forward not only to swimming in the ocean, but to the great rides on the Ocean Park amusement pier. I was especially looking forward to the airplanes. The airplanes were out on the end of the pier. They were large, two-passenger planes that were tethered by cables to a high steel tower. The cables were connected to a shaft in the tower that was turned by an electric motor. The airplanes would "fly" in a circle, faster and faster as the electric motor that turned the shaft built up speed. At top speed, the airplanes would sail out away from the tower, beyond the end of the pier, so that with a little imagination you would actually believe you were flying above the Pacific Ocean on, say, a strafing run or simply banking into a turn to get back to your carrier. There was an unconfirmed rumor that one of the cables snapped once, sending a young woman to her death. Her airplane was supposed to have been sent crashing into the surf. Whether this story was true or not it made the adventure all the more thrilling.

We rode the airplanes, the roller coaster and ferris wheel, had a hot dog, then went swimming briefly in the cold ocean. It was a great day. I loved the stink of seaweed, the white crust of salt on my skin, even the busy sand flies. The jellyfish, which were out in abundance that day, made me feel sick to my stomach, but I was fascinated by them, too. When William found one stranded on the beach, he'd turn it over with a stick. Right side up they were merely exotic-looking, but upside down they made you want to puke.

Meat flowers, I thought. "Meat flowers," I said.

"Slimy bastards, you mean," William said.

Slimy bastards, slimy bastards, I thought. "Slimy bastards," I said.

"They look like someone's insides," William said.

I thought of my insides. How could they look like upside-down jellyfish? I saw myself lying on the beach, my belly open, my insides melting in the sun. *Why do we have to have insides?* I thought. "Why do we have to have insides?" I said.

"So we can shit and fart," William said. "Why do you think?"

Shit and fart, I thought. "Shit and fart? Is that all they're for?"

"Piss and fuck, too," William said thoughtfully.

"Piss and fuck," I said. "Piss and fuck," I whispered.

"Piss you know about," William said. "Fuck will come later."

Sometimes his apparent sophistication annoyed me. "I know about it," I said. "I know about it."

"A man of experience," William said.

We were on the beach, near the pier. Two boys were leaning on the pilings. They were wearing Levis and white T-shirts. Both had bleached-blond crew cuts.

"Where's your zoot suit, spic?" one of them said.

They both laughed. The remark had been meant for William. His black Indian hair glistened in the hazy sunlight. He took a pack of Camels out of his shirt pocket and lit one up. This surprised me. I hadn't seen him smoke before.

"Hey, pachuco," the boy said. "Where's your zoot suit? You deaf or something?"

"Your mother sucks off donkeys," William said.

I started edging back up the beach, expecting William to do the same, but he didn't move. He stood there, casually tapping the ash off his Camel, facing the two bleached-blond crew cuts.

"We'd better go," I said. "We'd better go," I whispered.

One of the boys was taller than William, the other one heavier. They walked up to him, thumbs hooked into their front pockets.

"What was that, shithead?" the boy who was doing all the talking said. His face was studded with hard gray boils.

"I said your mother sucks off anything on four legs," William said.

It happened so fast that for a full second I didn't believe it happened at all. The red-faced boy had made a movement toward William, but before the movement could gather momentum, William hit him in the face. The sound was the sound of a raw potato being snapped in half by strong hands. The boy fell down, holding his face, blood spreading down his chin and onto his shirt. Before the other boy could move, William hit him in the stomach. He folded over and went down, curling into himself, his mouth wide but making no sound.

"Let's go," William said.

He slipped the roll of zinc pennies into his pocket. I hadn't seen him take them out. I guess the bleached-blond boys hadn't either.

"Are you coming, or what?" William said.

I was too stunned to move. My mind was spinning. This was my cousin William, but he was suddenly a stranger, capable of unimaginable things. I wasn't sure it was safe to be with him.

"My nose, my *nose*," moaned the bleeding boy. The other boy was still writhing soundlessly in the damp sand.

I followed behind William for a while, finally catching up to him at the train station. We had to wait for fifteen minutes for our train. I kept looking around, expecting the two bleached blonds to come after us.

"What are you so nervous about?" William said. He lit up another Camel and blew smoke at me. He looked annoyed and distracted. I noticed that the skin of the knuckles on his right hand was broken and bleeding.

I shrugged. I wanted a cigarette, though I knew the smoke would choke me. I didn't want to smoke it, I wanted to hold it. With a cigarette dangling casually in your mouth, you could never look afraid. A smoker always looks calm. He looks as if he's able to think clearly in any given situation. A smoker always has time to think things out. Pressure doesn't get to him. The smoker's squint was a fearless squint.

"I wish I could smoke," I said, whispering it again.

"You're too young," William said. "You start smoking at your age, you'll never get any taller. You'll be a midget all your life. How would you like to spend the rest of your life staring into belt buckles? You could get in the way of a tit and get your eye put out. It's a real hazard being short, Tryg."

"When did you start smoking?" I asked. "When did you start smoking?"

"I heard you the first time. What's with you, kid? You becoming some kind of whispering nut?"

I shrugged, embarrassed at my unshakable habit.

"I started smoking when I was about eleven," he said.

"But—"

He interrupted me. "But I grew anyway. That's because I don't inhale. Inhaling is what screws you up."

"I won't inhale then," I said, hating the whispering echo that passed over my lips unwilled.

"Naw. You'd inhale. You're the type to inhale. You're the type that screws himself up. If you could make yourself a midget, you would."

I couldn't tell if he was only joking or if he was serious. Either way, I felt insulted. "What do *you* know?" I said. "What do *you* know?" I regretted my tone, recalling the two boys lying under the Santa Monica pier. William could look at you in a deadpan way and you could never be sure about him.

"It's not that complicated, Tryg," he said, reasonably. "It's not that hard to figure people out. I read you easy as the Sunday comics. This is free advice, Tryg. You'd better take it."

"Hah!" I said loudly, alarming myself. "Hah," I whispered carefully.

William grabbed the back of my neck and shook me a little. He laughed then, mussing my hair.

The fifteen minutes were unending. The sun had gone down, and while it was still in the seventies, I was shivering. I had wanted to walk up Ocean Park Boulevard to the Douglas plant where my mother and Aunt Ginger worked, but that would have to wait for another time.

Then I saw the Big Red Car gliding down the tracks toward us.

William cracked a fart.

"Gone with the wind," I said. "Gone with the wind."

"Realistic" was one of Mitchell Selfage's favorite words. "Let's be realistic about this war," he said. "Does it really matter who wins it?"

Mother and Aunt Ginger looked at him as if he'd just spilled gasoline on a baby. "What are you saying?" Mother said. "Did you hear him say that?" she asked Aunt Ginger. "Maybe he wants the Japs over here raping us and tossing children up in the air so that they can catch them on their bayonets."

Mitchell posed with his cigarette, allowing smoke to drift out of his nostrils. "Do you believe everything you read, darling?" he said. He looked like Zachary Scott working Joan Crawford into a corner. "The propaganda machines of both sides tend to get carried away. They've got to keep the folks on the home front worked up. Otherwise, why would anyone want to send their boys into battle?"

"What about the newsreels?" Mother said. "I've *seen* what they did in Burma, and what the Nazis did in Poland."

"No you didn't," Mitchell said blandly. "You saw what they wanted you to see. You saw carefully staged propaganda. Besides, do you honestly believe the Americans and British treat the Japanese or Germans with loving Christian charity? Atrocity is part and parcel of the war process, my dears."

"Then why bother to fight at all?" Mother said.

"Oh, the fighting *is* necessary, don't misunderstand me. It's just that it's not over the issues the propaganda machine would have us believe."

"What *is* it over then?" Mother said. She was getting irritated, not so much at the outrageous thing Mitchell was saying but by his relentless air of superiority. She lit a cigarette and sucked at it thoughtfully. Aunt Ginger was only half listening to the conversation. She was sitting next to the window, looking out on the street, her mind drifting across the centuries. She was humming softly.

"What wars are always fought over," Mitchell said. "The constant struggle for markets. Our expansionary programs are in direct conflict with Japanese expansionary programs. Period. That's it. End of statement. As for the Germans, they simply want their empire back. To get it, they have to push the English, French, Dutch, and whomever else, out of the way."

"You make it seem so dirty and small-minded," Mother said.

"Exactly," Mitchell said. "That's exactly what it is."

"No reason for you to go, then," Aunt Ginger said. Her tone wasn't sarcastic or in any way mean. She said it dreamily and in an offhand manner. She was probably recalling some previous life where war was romantic and conducted for things like glory and honor, not market expansion.

"What is that supposed to mean?" Mitchell said.

"What do you think it means," Mother said. "It means you're doing a good job of talking yourself out of enlisting."

Mitchell scoffed loudly. "I don't have to *talk* myself out of anything. I'm not going to be 'embarrassed' into becoming gun fodder for the likes of Roosevelt and his big-money friends."

"President Roosevelt is a very great man," Aunt Ginger said.

"So the propaganda machine would have you believe."

It was a Sunday morning in late winter. William was out in the alley with his B B rifle, shooting at blackbirds on telephone wires. I had just finished reading the comics and was on my way into the bedroom to see what was happening on the shortwave bands. I stopped to listen to Mitchell's assessment of World War II.

His arguments were depressing, even though I didn't believe him. *No, no,* I thought to myself. *The war isn't like that at all. The Japanese and the Germans are evil and must be destroyed, otherwise they will destroy us.*

"Whispering Smith," Mitchell said. He gave me a scathing look. Once again I had revealed my inmost thoughts without realizing I was doing it. My face got hot. Mitchell got up and went into the bathroom. He came back with a roll of medical adhesive tape. He cut off a strip with his pocket knife and put it over my mouth. "We're going to put an end to this nonsense once and for all," he said.

"What do you think you're doing?" Mother said. She got up off the sofa and came toward me. Mitchell caught her arm.

"He whispers and repeats," Mitchell said. "There's something wrong with him. I think we should stop it."

"Not like that, we won't," Mother said. She peeled the tape off my mouth. Mitchell grabbed the tape out of her hand and covered my mouth with it again.

"It's the only way. He needs a constant reminder. It's a bad habit now, but it could develop into some kind of dementia."

Mother peeled the tape off again. This time she wadded it up and threw it into a wastebasket. Mitchell calmly cut another length of tape and pressed it over my lips.

"I think I know what I'm doing. I studied behavioral psychology for two semesters at the University."

"I don't care what you studied. You're not going to tape Trygve's mouth. It's inhuman."

She yanked the tape off my lips. I yelped.

Mother looked at Mitchell with disgust. "You enjoy humiliating him, don't you?"

"Good grief!" Mitchell said. "Be realistic. I only want the boy to adjust. He's got to adjust, you know. Otherwise, I think he should go back to his grandparents."

I was thunderstruck. I picked up a piece of discarded tape and put it over my mouth. They didn't notice me do this. Their argument distracted them. With my mouth sealed shut under adhesive tape, I went into the bedroom and switched on the shortwave receiver, volume turned up to drown out any thoughts of northern Montana and my grandparents' house.

↓

With Rio De Janeiro thumping sambas in my headset and my mouth taped shut, uncalled-for memories were released from their locked-up places. The faintly medicinal smell of the adhesive tape, Mitchell Selfage's threat to send me back to Montana, triggered with a clarity I hadn't experienced before the image of Mother stepping into the black car parked in my grandparents' driveway. I was out in a field, a quarter mile away. She had come to stay, I'd thought, and I'd never been happier. The man she was with was tall and dark with a hooked nose. He wore a suit at all times, even at breakfast, and his fingernails were perfectly trimmed. And even if she hadn't come to stay, then surely she would take me with her when she left. But there she was in her flowered dress and white shoes, stepping into the black car. The man wore a hat, and he waved at me in the field as the car headed down the dirt road that led into town. I chased the car, screaming at the top of my lungs, chased it even after I could no longer see it. Later that same day, I killed myself.

At least that's what I wanted my grandparents to believe. I wanted them to be sorry. I wanted them to grieve for what had been done to me. They left me alone in the house that afternoon. Grandmother had to drive Grandfather to the medical center for treatment—a regular trip they made once a month. I didn't like my grandparents very much, but they were all I had. And now I had to watch them drive away from me, too, leaving me alone in the old house, nothing but wind-moan for company.

I couldn't stand being alone. Fear and then anger made me take desperate measures. I found Grandmother's largest butcher knife and wondered for a long time how it would feel as it pierced the skin between my ribs and then my heart. I took off my shirt and held the steel point against my pale skin. Then I remembered a movie I'd seen where the sound of a knife penetrating a man's back was *crunchy*. I may or may not have been able to stand the pain, but I knew I couldn't bear to hear that *crunch*.

So I drove the point of the knife into a flat board about six inches square. I used some medical adhesive tape to attach the board to my chest. I put on my shirt—the effect was chilling. A large, heavy-handled butcher knife had been driven square into the middle of my small chest. Dead, I knew I looked dead. To make it all the more authentic, I spread half a bottle of ketchup over my shirt at the point of penetration.

Then I laid down in the middle of the kitchen floor and waited for them to come home.

But I was defeated by Norwegian fatalism. If they were surprised to see their murdered grandson lying on the kitchen floor, their unimpressed expressions did not betray their feelings. Through squinted eyes I saw them go about their business. Grandmother had been to the grocery store and she busied herself putting cans and jars into the cupboards. Grandfather scratched his ribs thoughtfully and yawned. If I had started to rot he wouldn't have wrinkled his nose. "Looks like only two for supper tonight, hey?" he said. Then, without waiting for an answer, he shuffled out of the kitchen on his rigid legs.

Grandmother turned the radio on for the Polka Hour. She heated the morning's coffee and poured herself a cup. She took out her crochet work and began to hum along with the polkas.

I knew I looked perfectly dead, and I wasn't going to give up that easily. Eventually a fly would land on my face and I would allow it to crawl into my grotesquely opened mouth. Surely that

would support beyond question my claim on death. But no help-
ful fly came by. After another half hour or so, the high-spirited
accordians began to soften my will.

My back was sore. My crotch itched. I blinked.

I got up slowly, trying to prevent my shifting weight from
making the floor creak. I eased my way out of the kitchen.

"Soak that shirt," my grandmother said.

↓

I saw the woman give Mitchell a quick kiss on the cheek. When
he came back to the truck, he saw me looking at him oddly. "Don't
worry about it," he said. "She's my Cousin Millie."

His Cousin Millie lived off Wilshire, near MacArthur Park, a
long way from his milk route. After we had roast-beef sandwiches
at Don the Beachcomber's, we drove for half an hour without
making one delivery. We stopped at a small stucco cottage covered
with bougainvillea vines. The house seemed to be on fire with the
bright red blossoms. Mitchell went in and stayed for more than
an hour. He'd brought in a case full of butter, cream, and eggs.

"Millie's husband is in North Africa," Mitchell explained. "He's
with the Tank Corps. Millie gets a government allotment but she
needs a little extra, for the children. I guess they're your second
cousins." He slapped my shoulder as if to congratulate me for
having this category of relatives.

We drove to Cousin Millie's house every third or fourth Saturday. I hated to sit in the parked truck for the hour he spent with
his Cousin Millie. Sometimes, out of boredom, I'd take a walk.
I'd walk to MacArthur Park and visit the bird sanctuary. The big
black statue of Prometheus always fascinated me. It stood at the
park entrance, like a giant guardian of the mysteries to be found
inside. When I walked past the statue, I felt the hair on the back
of my neck stiffen. I didn't relax again until I found the birds.

There were always a lot of soldiers and sailors strolling in the park with girls. Sometimes I'd see them lying together on the grass, kissing and petting without any self-consciousness. That was because of the war. Chances were good that the soldiers and sailors wouldn't be coming back. They thought of themselves as dead men. Goners. Those marked for death couldn't be concerned with propriety or caution. It wouldn't have made sense. I understood this. I'd imagined being free of self-consciousness myself. There was a prerequisite though. You had to be marked for death. It was an agreeable trade-off. Being marked for death gave you a jauntiness and openness ordinary citizens could only dream of. All the sailors and soldiers I saw with their girlfriends in MacArthur Park had this jauntiness and openness. It made them godlike. I knew that their neck hairs did not stiffen when they passed under the blank stare of Prometheus. They, like the eight-foot-tall god, were above small-minded human worries.

When I almost stumbled over a sailor and a girl lying behind an oleander bush, it didn't surprise me at all that they did not stop what they were doing. I was the one who was embarrassed. "Sorry," I said. "Sorry," I whispered. I backed away from them. But they didn't acknowledge my intrusion at all. They were locked in a tight bare-legged embrace. I fell over myself getting away from them.

I was obsessed with "suicide mission" movies. The sub that has to slip past the iron sub nets to get into Tokyo Bay so that it can pave the way for an air attack. The single fighter aircraft, flying a one-way trip into Germany to save the underground resistance movement. The marine radio man asked by his commanding officer to set his rig up on a hill to signal for air support, even though the battalion would have to leave him stranded when they pulled out.

When Mitchell was visiting Cousin Millie, I played out such scenes. I was the one marked for death. With great relish, I adopted a tragic view of myself. After passing under the watchful gaze of Prometheus, I'd shove my hands into my pockets and saunter through the park among the strolling couples. I, no less than they, was a goner. I walked heavily on the heels of my feet, disdaining Mitchell's gliding, balls-first gait. If the soldiers and sailors and their girlfriends saw me, they saw one of themselves. They saw Charlie Jones, Bill Tucker, Jerry Granger, Buddy Thompson, someone above the petty concerns of those who would live to ripe old ages.

I loved the pose. I loved being someone everyone could like. To encourage this view of myself, I had to make it real. To make it real required a strong and unwavering imaginative act. I had to elaborate the details of my coming death in combat. This was important. I had to work at it. I couldn't afford to be slack on the details.

Back in the milk truck, sitting in the driver's seat, I saw gouts of blood spurting from my chest. I smelled the acrid smoke of my burning airplane. I held the steering wheel tightly, jerked it back and forth fighting a massive instability in the damaged control system of my B-17. I felt myself passing out, felt the big plane sink into a deadly stall. Still, the relentless German fighters came at us, cannons winking in the twilit sky. My co-pilot, Larry Kinkaid, was dead. His head lolled limply against the backrest of his seat. His eyes had a melancholy stare.

It was hard to maintain such fantasies in the bright springtime afternoons of Los Angeles. You could only lose so much blood. You could gaze into the melancholy eyes of your dead co-pilot only for so long.

Once when Mitchell was taking an especially long time with Cousin Millie, I decided to go knock on the door. It had been nearly an hour and a half. I'd gone through my best marked-for-death fantasies several times each. They were wearing thin.

I knocked lightly, then harder, but no one answered. I tried the door and it opened on silent hinges. The radio was playing dance band music, but the house seemed empty. Walking on the balls of my feet, I toured the kitchen and a small dining room, then went down a hallway. The house was full of geegaws. Every room had shelves full of porcelain dolls and animals, little manger scenes, painted dishes from the World's Fair, trumpet-blowing angels, souvenirs of all kinds. I stopped at a slightly ajar door at the end of the carpeted hallway. I listened for a while at the cracked door but could only hear the dance band. I pushed the door open a few more inches and peeked inside.

Mitchell was lying fully clothed on the bed, his legs crossed at the ankles. He was smoking a cigarette. Millie was sitting on the edge of the bed. She was dressed in a bathrobe and had one leg crossed over the other. She was looking at her foot. The toes were splayed and I could smell the sharp odor of nail polish. Her toenails were glossy red.

Somewhere in North Africa, Millie's husband's tank was lumbering up and down the white hot dunes. I could almost see his red, sunburnt face, his bloodshot eyes. Mitchell reached out absentmindedly and touched Millie's arm. She smiled.

I backed down the hallway on the balls of my feet, one careful foot behind the other until I made the living room, where my elbow nudged a shelf full of geegaws. A porcelain angel toppled and fell. I caught it before it hit the floor but my desperate grip cracked its trumpet. The bell of the trumpet snapped and sailed off, hitting a metal heat register. It broke into several pieces. I shoved the pieces into the heat register and put the hornless angel back on its shelf.

Back in the truck I opened myself a half pint of chocolate milk.

Millie had seen me. I didn't have any doubt I had been noticed, but I could have been one of her geegaws, judging from the look in her eyes. It was a matter of indifference to her. She was a woman my mother would have called "cheap" because her yellow hair had inch-long black roots. But her amazingly cool green eyes were not cheap. They were the unperturbed eyes of a goner. Millie had the "marked-for-death" look that so many soldiers and sailors had.

That was why it didn't matter to her that I saw her sitting on the bed in her bathrobe with Mitchell lying beside her.

That was why she'd winked at me.

↓

"There's always something," I thought. Then I said it. It was my way of defeating the need to repeat myself. If it started out as a *thought*, then, when I repeated it, people would only have to hear it *once*. When I spoke to people, I "thought" my responses first. The only trouble with this strategy was that it made me hesitate before speaking. To make this hesitation seem justified, I tried to appear thoughtful. Before speaking, I would knit my brow, or rub my hand over my hair vigorously, as if carefully selecting my words.

Aunt Ginger sipped her coffee. "I know, Tryg," she said.

I liked Aunt Ginger because she understood me even though I couldn't say what was in my mind—not to my satisfaction, at least.

"Because, if you're *dead,* and it's all black and empty, well, that just can't last forever." I thought it then said it, but it still wasn't exactly what I wanted to say.

"Death be not proud," Aunt Ginger said, stirring sugar into her cup.

I rubbed my hair vigorously, knitted my brow. "Because there just always has to be *some*thing, even if the sun blows up and the earth and moon turn into smoke."

"Yes, yes, Tryg, that's right," Aunt Ginger said. Her eyes, usually so dreamy, were electrified with excitement.

I felt encouraged. "I'm me and you're you," I said. "But if I wasn't me and you weren't you, then someone would be here instead of us, talking just like this, and it could even be us, ourselves, though it doesn't really matter."

I was confusing myself, but I believed what I said. Aunt Ginger reached across the breakfast table and squeezed my hand. "Maybe we are always here as ourselves with no choice at all," she said gravely. I saw a quick tear start out of her eye.

William got up and grunted irritably. He cleared the table and put the dishes into the sink with a sharp clatter. The three of us had just eaten a late breakfast. Mother and Mitchell had taken the Cadillac for a drive up the coast, which made me anxious. They promised to be back for dinner, though, and reminding myself of that calmed me a bit. It was a bright Saturday in May. There'd been a wonderful article in the paper about the battle, last year, in the Coral Sea. Six Jap planes had tried to land on the *Yorktown,* an American carrier. The pilots, confused after the heat of battle and in poor weather, mistook the *Yorktown* for one of their own carriers and were destroyed one by one as they tried to put down. In that same battle, the Japanese carrier, the *Shoho,* was sunk in ten minutes by Dauntless Dive Bombers and Devastators, a torpedo bomber also made by Douglas.

I felt elated! Dauntless Dive Bombers! The planes Mother and Aunt Ginger riveted! I'd pointed the news item out to Aunt Ginger, but it hadn't seemed to interest her very much.

"The dead are burying the dead," she said, cryptically.

I didn't know what she meant, but she reminded me of the problem I'd been working over in my mind earlier that morning while lying in bed listening to the Saturday morning radio programs.

Fantasizing my death in combat over and over led me to think about what death would feel like after you were killed and your heart stopped beating. I didn't think much of heaven and the angels, mainly because I couldn't picture them. Heaven was a vague place, too clean and white to be very interesting. What could you possibly do in a place like that where the centuries ticked by like seconds? The potential for boredom was mind boggling. I couldn't visualize The Supreme Being very well in this cloudy, angel-infested place. At best he was an old man on a gold throne, like Washington or Lincoln, only dressed in pure white, dozing on his arm while a hundred angels played lullabies on their silver harps. I just couldn't get interested in heaven, angels, or The Supreme Being. What interested me was the problem of death. *There* was the whole mystery. If you died, what came next? Nothing at all? But that didn't make sense. You were "dead" before you were born, but there was a complete *world* before you were born and it was being seen and felt and lived in by "someone." How could being "dead" cancel out all that richness? I invented a private catechism to help me zero in on the problem of death:

>Trygve Soren Napoli *was* dead and he will *be* dead again.
>But the world keeps being a world, Trygve or no Trygve.
>What if everyone in the world were dead?
>But that couldn't be seen or felt. The only thing that can be seen or felt is life.
>So there is no such thing as everyone in the world being dead.
>Maybe before the universe was created there was nothing at all for millions of billions of trillions of years.
>But that didn't mean anything because there was no one around who had to wait for the universe to happen.
>Millions of billions of trillions of years would be the same thing as a millionth of a second if there were no one around to keep track of the time.
>So there is never nothing.
>There is always something.
>Whether Trygve Soren Napoli was around or not.
>Whether Charles Jones, Bill Tucker, Bob Smith, or Jerry Granger were around or not.
>Whether the six Jap pilots who tried to land on the *Yorktown* were around or not.

After breakfast I went to Azad's house. He answered my knock, but kept me waiting on the porch. "Let's go listen to the radio," I said.

"Not now," he said. "My mother is not yet dressed."

We fooled around on the lawn. The Yaznurs didn't keep their yard up and the grass was yellow and long. Azad was in a quiet mood. We wrestled around on the lawn for a while. He let me pin him without putting up much of a struggle. Then his mother, a stout, black-haired woman, came out with a tray of cookies and lemonade.

"Were we dead before we were born?" I thought, then said.

"What?" Azad said. He looked confused. His big round eyes were like wet chocolate.

"I don't think there can be such a thing as death," I said.

"Yehs, there is dith," he said.

I smiled indulgently at his foreign simple-mindedness. I knitted my brow. "No, not really, Azad. See, if you are dead, well, it's just Azad that's dead."

He looked at me, his soft brown eyes hardening. "Stupeed," he said, drawing the word out. "You don't know dith. You never have seen dith."

I shrugged, rubbed my hair vigorously. "So?" I said. "I suppose *you* have seen it?"

"Yehs, I have seen."

"A man of experience," I said, mimicking William's cutting style.

"They shitted my father," Azad said.

"Shitted?"

"Shotted. Shotted him yehs, dead, smack in the head."

"Shot you mean," I said. "Shot you mean," I whispered, forgetting for the moment my technique.

Azad held up his finger as if it were a gun and said, "Bang," his distracted eyes reliving the scene. "The German man shotted him."

I flinched. I was afraid of him suddenly. He seemed older than me, more experienced. "Let's go listen to the radio," I said.

We went into his bedroom. As we passed by the kitchen, Azad's mother looked at me with enormous anger in her eyes. I was glad to get into the bedroom where the radio was. Azad switched it on and tuned to the thirty-meter band. London came booming in. Big Ben chimed and an English voice told us, importantly, Greenwich Mean Time.

↓

A new family moved into the apartment building, the Bruckners. "Jews," Mitchell said. "Not only Jews, but Jews with kids. Wait till Hobarth hears about this."

Hobarth was the landlord. The apartment we lived in was "restricted." A sign outside said this in small, meticulously printed letters. "Restricted" meant that white Christians were the only acceptable tenants.

"Who's going to tell him?" Mother said. "You?"

"No one will have to tell him a thing. All he's got to do is look at them. I'd say the Sturdevants are going to have to do some fast talking."

The Sturdevants were the managers of the apartment building. They only received forty dollars a month for the job and so were not strict enforcers of the landlord's rules. Besides, the Sturdevants themselves had a six-year-old boy.

"They seem very nice," Aunt Ginger said.

Mitchell scoffed. "Why wouldn't they seem nice? If you were a Jew in a restricted apartment wouldn't you want to seem nice? Would you play your Mickey Katz records with the volume turned up high or dance the hora in the halls?"

"This is 1943, for God's sakes," Mother said.

"Jews are Jews, Gentiles are Gentiles, 1943 or 1953. What's the year got to do with it?" Mitchell said.

We were at the dinner table, finishing up dessert. Dessert was my birthday cake. I had just turned eleven. Eleven seemed like a magic number. I felt that I had a chance to leave childhood behind. Eleven was a doorway.

Mother sighed wearily. She'd cooked a rib roast and a birthday cake after coming home from work. It was now past eight. William and I were going to see a new Bela Lugosi movie at the Variety. We had an hour before the second show. It was a Friday night and there was a full moon out. My stomach was already anticipating the horrors to come. Still, I had a second piece of cake.

Malcolm Bruckner was coming with us. William and I met him that afternoon and when we told him about the new Dracula movie he asked if he could come along. Malcolm was twelve years old. He had a wide smile with big spaces between his teeth. He was a lot taller than me but shorter than William.

William and I had shown him the fort and explained the whistle-warning system. We told him how the children had to run out the back door of the apartment building whenever the landlord showed up. The notion that the children were fugitives interested him.

"What happens if we get caught?" he asked.

"You don't," William said ominously.

"You just *don't*," I echoed, my brow knitted, evidently by the seriousness of our situation as illegal residents.

"Sure, but what *if?*" Malcolm persisted.

William drew a finger across his throat, as if it were the blade of a knife.

After the movie the three of us walked home under the bone-white moon. The movie was replaying itself in my mind. Something about it made perfect sense to me, but I couldn't exactly tell myself what it was. It had to do with the problem I was having with death. A vampire was a thing that was dead but was also immortally alive.

It seemed just the thing I was looking for. A vampire fed on the living so that it could remain immortal. Wasn't that exactly what I had been trying to say about the "thing" that always survives the death of a single person? The single person dies, but something keeps seeing and feeling the world. This thing is immortal, even when the sun blows up and the planets burn. Because when there is nothing, there isn't even the sense of nothing. Nothing is just that: nothing. The vampire is the seer and feeler that flies across the centuries, unchanged. The vampire is in us, gradually bleeding our lives away, but also giving us a kind of immortality.

"Wake up, Tryg," William said, grabbing my neck.

I had stepped into traffic on Adams Boulevard paying no attention to the traffic lights.

I rubbed my head with both hands vigorously. "If you're

dead, see," I said, "well that's just like when the vampire has to go back into his coffin when the sun is up."

"Jesus Christ," William said. "Can't you talk about something else for a change? You give me the creeps, you and my stepmother, yakking about death all the goddamned time."

"Actually," I said, still thinking out loud, "a vampire isn't alive *or* dead. For a vampire, being alive and being dead are the same thing."

"If you don't shut up I'm going to drop you into a storm drain," William said.

"Does he always talk like this?" Malcolm said. "What is he, some kind of nut case?"

Malcolm was from back east somewhere and his accent amused us. William laughed. "He's a case of nuts, all right," he said. "He's an orchard full of nuts."

They didn't bother me. In fact, I sort of enjoyed them talking about me as if I weren't there. I felt absent, and I felt honored in my absence.

"Hey, Monk," Malcolm said. "Are you nutso?"

William laughed. Malcolm started dancing around me, touching me on the arm, as if he were sparring or playing tag.

"Monk," William said. "Hey, that's good, Malcolm. Monk. That's him, all right."

It was different than being called Young Mister Napoli on the school grounds. I liked being called "Monk." It went with being talked about as if I weren't there. I felt honored.

William later amended this to "The Monk." If he was irritated with me for, say, practicing Morse code in bed by hissing out series of dots and dashes, he'd say, "The Monk is driving me crazy," or "The Monk is about to be kicked out of bed."

I didn't mind. Having a special nickname went along with being eleven. I was dimly aware that I was growing toward new possibilities. It didn't matter that these new possibilities were a little strange. The important thing was that I was changing, and that the changes made me feel unconfined. If the changes caused me to grow bat wings under a full moon, I didn't mind.

We walked up Adams to Ridgely Drive, turned up Ridgely

and headed for our apartment building. William and Malcolm were walking a few paces ahead of me. I heard William say, "Hey, Malc, who was that girl with the big tits I saw you talking to out by the incinerators today?"

"You mean Betty?" Malcolm said. "Betty's my sister."

"Oh," William said.

"It's okay," Malcolm said. "She's proud of her tits. You should see her tits. Cantaloupes."

Bela Lugosi looked at the tits of the girl he attacked, but it was a quick, almost embarrassed glance. His black tongue flicked out once, but then he went to work on her throat. She went rigid, her eyes popped open, and she made a little noise before she died.

I had the crazy idea that she was enjoying it. Which proved, in my mind, that I *was* a nut case.

Monk, the Nut. I flapped my arms over my head like wings and made a nutty sound. Both William and Malcolm looked back at me and shook their heads. "The kid is hopeless," William said.

↓

Franchot Tone came to dinner. Except, just as I'd thought, he wasn't really Franchot Tone. He was Jack Twilly, Franchot Tone's handyman. At least that's what he told us.

"I never said I was anybody but Jack Twilly," he said to Mother, explaining the series of events that led up to his being invited to dinner. "Your old man here pulled a boner."

"The thing is," Mitchell said, "Jack is a set carpenter down at Warner Brothers. Jack knows Mr. Tone and a lot of other stars."

"Oh Jesus yes," Jack Twilly said, laughing. "I know the bums. I know a lot of them."

"He calls them bums," Mitchell said, marveling at Jack Twilly's insider status.

"Just kidding, Mrs. Selfage. Hell, most of them are damn

fine guys and gals, contrary to what you might have read in the gossip rags."

"Jack helped build the set for *Captains Courageous*," Mitchell said.

"Well, it's my trade, carpentry is," Jack Twilly said, modestly.

"See, that's what he was doing out at Franchot Tone's house," Mitchell explained to Mother. "He was building some cabinets for Mr. Tone's gun collection."

"Say, listen," Jack Twilly said. "I've done a little acting, too."

This was news to Mitchell. He set his coffee cup down too hard, chipping the saucer. "Really?" he said. "You're not pulling my leg again, are you, Jack?"

Jack Twilly leaned forward on the table, frowning. "I don't pull anybody's leg, Mitch," he said. Then, winking at Mother, he added, "Unless it's hooked onto a lady good-looking as this."

Mother got up from the table and picked up the dirty dishes. She went into the kitchen. I could hear her sigh above the running tap water.

"Well let us in on it, Jack. What movies did you appear in?" Mitchell asked eagerly.

Jack Twilly squinted at the ceiling, recalling his many acting jobs. "Did you happen to catch *The Sign of the Cross* a few years back? Starring Claudette Colbert?"

"Sure!" Mitchell said. "*You* were in that? That was no 'B' movie. That was an 'A.' I think I paid a dollar and a quarter to see it at the Pantages."

"Right. Well, I was what they call a 'costume extra.' You remember the milk bath scene, where Claudette gets into a tub full of milk?"

"Of course I do!" Mitchell said, thrilled. "How could anyone forget that scene!"

"The guy pouring milk into the tub—that was me, all duded up like a Roman palace eunuch."

"Well I'll be—" Mitchell said.

"I know what you're going to ask," Jack Twilly said. "You want to know if she was really in the raw, or did she have on her skivvies."

Jack Twilly sipped his coffee, letting the suspense build.

William had already left the table; I was getting ready to. But this last teasing bit of Hollywood insider talk glued me to my chair.

"Let it be known, gentlemen," Jack Twilly said, "that young Miss Colbert was naked as Eve."

"I thought—" Mitchell began.

"You thought the Hays Office was the watchdog over such goings-on. Well they are. Actually, the moviegoer didn't get to see very much. The typical moviegoer has got a pretty good imagination and most of them believed they saw a little titty nipple peeking over the milk bubbles. But the Hayes people went over the print with a magnifying glass and they passed it." He yawned and looked at his watch. "Well, I ought to be getting on the road. Mr. Tone wants me to put up some beech-wood book-cases for him tomorrow. He's quite the reader, you know. Most people think movie stars are all body and no brain. Not true. I say that from personal experience. Not true at all."

"Wait a minute," Mitchell said. "What about Claudette Colbert? I mean, did she just walk onto the set in the *raw*—is it that casual?"

Jack Twilly pinched his nose thoughtfully. "Mitch, there wasn't a man on the set who didn't have a rod-on—oh, sorry, Ginger, you're so quiet I forgot you were there."

Aunt Ginger was sitting between Mitchell and Jack Twilly, but she hadn't said anything during the entire meal. She now looked at Jack Twilly, a bewildered expression in her eyes.

"Forgot?" she said.

"I was just telling Mitch here about Claudette Colbert taking a bath in the raw. Hell, sure thing! We all saw her! Every red-blooded man on the set was ready to go to war. Except for the queens, of course."

"I saw that movie," Aunt Ginger said. "It was so sad."

"Yes, yes, it was a regular tear-jerker," Jack Twilly said.

"It was more like a memory than a movie," Aunt Ginger said.

Jack Twilly looked at her. "Uh-huh," he said. "I know what

you mean. That's when a movie is good, when it's like your own personal experience."

"Say, Jack," Mitchell said. "How do you get to be an extra, anyway?"

"Well, in my case, I just happened to be handy. Now, if you want to get some of that easy money, go down to Central Casting and fill out a form. You may be too good-looking, though, to wind up on a call sheet. They want characters, not leading men."

Mitchell seemed both flattered and disappointed.

"You mind if I take a couple of slices of that roast with me, Mitch?" Jack Twilly said.

Mitchell got up and went into the kitchen. He came back with a sheet of wax paper. He cut half a dozen generous slices of roast beef for Jack Twilly and wrapped them carefully in the wax paper.

"Where the bejesus do you people get meat like this, anyway?" Jack Twilly said.

Mitchell started to answer him, but Jack Twilly spoke first. "Oh, hell. I forgot. You're a milkman. You're up to your ears in the black market."

"Keep it on the Q.T., Jack," Mitchell said, winking.

"Oh, will I ever! How are you fixed for gas stamps, Mitch?" Mitchell winked.

"Listen. I'll make you a deal. I'll introduce you to Mr. Tone for a book of gas stamps. What do you say? Now, I can't guarantee he'll do anything for you, but I can get you as far as a handshake. How about it? I know you want to get into the flickers. And, frankly speaking, I think you're the type to make the grade."

Mitchell's eyes went a little glassy. He took a deep breath and leaned heavily on the table. "Mr. Twilly," he said, "we're in business."

↓

The school year ended on a sour note. One of the illegal cats in our apartment building was killed. A car ran over it. It was a big friendly tomcat we called Tarzan. William and I buried Tarzan out in the vacant lot where the fort was. After we buried the cat, we enlarged the fort. The fort was getting too small since the number of children in the apartment building was rising. Back in December there had been six; now, in June, there were at least nine, counting Malcom's sister Betty, but she refused to run to the fort when the warning whistle blew. It was beneath her dignity. Besides, she was tall and mature enough to "pass" for an adult. Whenever Mr. Hobarth came by in his big black Packard, Betty would stay in the apartment and play the piano. She was a wonderful pianist and since her parents both worked night shifts out at Lockheed, she played it mostly at night. Some people complained, but most didn't because she played so beautifully.

Using a pickax, William extended the main trench of the underground fort another five feet. He loosened the packed dirt with the pick, then shoveled it out. After about five hours of hard work, the job was done, except for the planks we needed to find to cover the new trench. When the planks were in place, we'd cover them with dirt, camouflaging the underground haven perfectly.

Betty and William went to the same high school. They didn't have much to say to each other, but I knew for a fact that William had a crush on her. The way he tensed up when he was within her sight—flexing his long thin arms dramatically, or spitting with artistic precision between his feet—gave him away.

Not that I blamed him. I had fallen in love with her too and had died bleeding in her arms many times in my imagination. Betty was pretty rather than beautiful, but it was her personality that was so beguiling. She was totally honest, refusing to make any compromise for appearance's sake. She had long curly black hair, hazel eyes that could look at anything for as long as they wanted to, and a wide band of freckles that ran from cheek to cheek, crossing the bridge of her nose like a small constellation of red-brown stars. And her breasts, just as Malcolm had told us, were big as cantaloupes.

I had seen them.

I'd been in the Bruckner apartment with Malcolm, playing Parcheesi. Mr. and Mrs. Bruckner had left for the Lockheed plant. It was about seven o'clock in the evening and we were getting ready to listen to the Lone Ranger.

"Monk," Malcolm said, scooping up the Parcheesi pieces as our program came on the radio, "I'd better warn you."

"What about?" I said, after first thinking it.

"My sister. She's different."

The Lone Ranger was beginning. I loved the beginning, the excited announcer saying, *A fiery horse with the speed of light, a cloud of dust, and a hearty hi-yo Silver—the Lone Ranger!* and the William Tell Overture trumpeting the arrival of the great masked man.

"Monk, listen to me a sec, will you?"

I turned up the volume on the Bruckners' big Zenith console model radio. "Hi-yo *Silver!*" the masked rider shouted.

Betty Bruckner came in and turned the radio down. "You're not going to play it full blast, you little warts," she said.

She'd just come out of the shower and was toweling herself. Other than the big bath towel, she had nothing else on. Her cantaloupe-round breasts flashed in front of my eyes as she leaned down to adjust the volume control. The big breasts with perfect nipples, hot pink from the shower, glistened. They peeked out from the towel, taking my breath away. They were like a dream of breasts, a memory too remote to be other than a dream. The rugged mass of black curls between her legs, revealed in heart-stopping glimpses, was beyond memory or dream. I turned away from her so quickly I knocked the Parcheesi set off the coffee table, scattering the pieces.

She walked out.

"Bad men on horseback kill banker," Tonto was saying, his voice Indian-flat.

"That's what I meant by different, Monk," Malcolm said.

I busied myself with the scattered Parcheesi set, and the thundering hoofbeats of my heart.

"A needless crime, Tonto," the Lone Ranger agreed.

↓

Uncle Gerald's ship had docked at Long Beach and we drove down to pick him up. The streets were full of sailors and soldiers, marching together in a mob-like way rather than a military way. Mitchell had to stop for groups of them every so often. When he stopped, the sailors and soldiers would look into the windows of the Cadillac as if they were searching for someone in particular.

"They're looking for Mexicans," Mitchell said. "This has been coming on for a few weeks now."

"You'd think they'd had enough of war," Mother said.

"Most of them are recruits. They're just working off their jitters."

"Why the Mexicans?" Aunt Ginger said.

"Not *all* Mexicans," Mitchell explained. "Just the gangs. The zoot-suiters. The boys just want to put an end to all the zoot-suit trouble."

The big car rocked a little as a group of sailors leaned against it. Mother and Aunt Ginger were up front with Mitchell. William and I had the back seat. A sailor was looking at William. William gave him the finger.

"This is a mean bunch," Mitchell said. He was getting nervous. Two soldiers were on the hood of the Cadillac, peering in at Mother and Aunt Ginger. They were giving them the wolfwhistle and rolling their eyes.

The sailor William had given the finger to was trying to yank open the door, but too many other sailors were pressed up against it.

"We'd better get out of here," Mother said.

"I can't. I'm blocked in," Mitchell said.

The back door suddenly swung open and the sailor was in the car on top of William. William kicked out at him and the sailor yelled for help.

"Drive the goddamned *car!*" I said, shocking myself. The sailor had William by the hair and was banging his head against the back of the seat. Mitchell finally got the car moving forward and the sailor, who was half in the car and half out, lost his footing. He let go of William's hair and William kicked him again, this time a solid blow to the chest. The sailor barked the air out of his lungs and slipped out of the car. William slammed the door shut and locked it. Aunt Ginger was on her knees in the front seat leaning into the back. "Are you all right, are you all right?" she said. Her face was wet and her mouth looked distorted. My heart was hammering. I felt sick.

"I'm better off than that swabbie," William said. "The dumb bastard was pounding my head on the seat cushion—you can't get hurt that way."

"You boys want to control your language back there?" Mitchell said. "Especially you, Trygve. You're a little young to be tossing out obscenities like that. Whom did you think you were talking to, anyway?"

"I don't know," I mumbled.

"Well, you'd better apologize. It won't do, Trygve. If I were a more provincial sort you'd get a sound beating for using that type of language, especially in the presence of ladies."

"Sorry," I said.

We got on Long Beach Boulevard and Mitchell opened it up to fifty miles an hour, well above the speed limit. He gripped the wheel with both hands and sat upright on the seat. I could see Mother tensing her shoulders as the car roared and swayed, but she didn't say anything. Aunt Ginger, sitting next to the door, looked out the window at the passing buildings.

"We've got plenty of time," Mother finally said.

"Don't tell me how to drive a car," Mitchell said. He increased the speed of the Cadillac by another ten miles an hour.

Visions of the foster home flashed in my mind. "Maybe we'd better slow down," I said.

"What did I just tell you, Trygve?" Mitchell said.

"I didn't use bad language," I said.

"That's not the point. The point is you're speaking out of turn—it's the same thing."

"No it isn't," I said. I was marveling at myself for saying these things. My voice sounded different. *I wasn't repeating myself.* It made me alert to the suddenness of change. Mitchell made the big car swerve from lane to lane as he passed slower traffic. He drove as if possessed. I guess the mob of soldiers and sailors had scared him and he was now reacting to it. You could almost smell the adrenaline seeping from his pores.

"Jesus," Mother sighed.

Mitchell glared at her, taking his eyes from the road for a split second. In that moment, he almost ran over a woman walking a dog. He swerved again and the tires moaned as the car almost tipped over.

"Why doesn't everybody just shut up?" Mitchell said.

He finally slowed down to ten miles per hour above the speed limit. Mother turned on the radio. Jo Stafford was singing "Again" on KFI. The song made Aunt Ginger come out of her trance. She sang along with Jo Stafford. *Again, this couldn't happen again,* she sang, her voice a breathy whisper.

Uncle Gerald was waiting for us at the navy landing at the bottom of Pico Avenue. "Where the hell have you been?" he asked.

Mitchell told him about the mob that had delayed us, but Uncle Gerald didn't look convinced. He was cold and angry and wanted a drink. He seemed wrapped in fog and salt air. He smelled of brine and petroleum. His eyes were tired but wide open, as if he'd been staring into the sea for days at the wakes of torpedoes.

He got into the back seat with William and me after tossing

his sea bag into the trunk. "No," he said. "No pleasantries yet. Let's stop off for a snort first, then we'll kiss hello."

Mitchell stopped at the first bar he saw, a place called Hair O' the Dog Saloon. "I wouldn't mind a drink myself," he said.

William and I waited in the car. Fog was collecting in the streets, giving the few streetlights spectral halos.

I felt a little uneasy being alone with William. I had secret knowledge about the girl he had a crush on: I had seen Betty Bruckner's tits. I had seen more than her tits. I'd seen it all, up close and from a distance, and I'd seen it more than once. Betty was absolutely nonchalant around Malcolm and me—as if we were no more than a pair of dead houseflies lying on the windowsill. She must have believed that the image of her fully adult body in our immature grade-school minds had no impact. We were "warts." "Hold it down, you warts, I'm trying to do my algebra," she'd say. Or "Get out of the icebox, warts, the chicken salad is for tomorrow." She would walk around the apartment in panties and bra, or just her panties, but more often, she wore neither. She moved from room to room with contemptuous ease. I wasn't able to look at her directly, but would only sneak glances when I thought it was safe. But if she caught me, she only had to look at me with those unfaltering hazel eyes and I would wrench my neck to avoid being turned into ashes.

William and I waited almost an hour in near silence before they came out of the bar. Uncle Gerald had his arms around both Aunt Ginger and Mother. He was singing in a hoarse baritone. While he looked festive, the others looked gloomy. Mitchell got behind the wheel of the Cadillac and started the engine. He depressed the starter pedal too long. The scream of shearing metal rose above the eight-cylinder roar. "Goddamn son of a bitch," Mitchell said, his face white as candle wax in the streetlight's thin aura.

"Easy does it," Uncle Gerald said. "Nothing's gained in this man's navy by calling down God's wrath."

They were all sitting up front. Aunt Ginger sat in Uncle Gerald's lap, facing sideways toward Mitchell.

"Take it easy or I'm walking," Mother said as Mitchell let out the clutch too quickly and the car lurched forward.

"God but it's good to be back," Uncle Gerald said, his voice trembling. Aunt Ginger pulled his head to her breast and stroked his hair. But later that night, back at the apartment, Uncle Gerald became sullen and abusive and called Aunt Ginger "nickle-and-dime whore" and "common slut" until she cried, and when she cried he twisted her arm to make her stop. "Bloody public pump," he said, his teeth clenched, his drunk eyes punishing and blind.

↓

We all drove up the coast for a picnic. We stopped at a quiet spot north of Ventura. Uncle Gerald had sworn off drinking for a while and was in an upbeat though somewhat pensive mood. That was fine by me. William and I spread out the blankets and then carried baskets of food and drink down from the car.

It was a fantastic, unblemished spot, cupped by high cliffs. Miles of clean white sand shored the endless, west-reaching ocean. The warm breeze stank with the keen brine-and-seaweed smell I had come to love. I walked down to the wet sand to look for shells. Uncle Gerald came along with me.

"I hope you're not going to grow up thinking badly of me, Tryg old man," he said.

His friendly tone of voice embarrassed me. "Oh no," I said.

"I realize I can be a tad unpleasant at times." He stood facing the sea, his back to me. He was a big, squarely built man with thick black hair that waved over his massive head in heavy, gleaming locks. As he talked, he kept his hands folded behind his back. They were big, meaty hands, heavily veined and knuckled. I couldn't believe a man with such hands could allow himself to punch a beautiful woman in the face. I saw in my mind the blow that had lifted Aunt Ginger off her feet and flung her down in a sobbing heap; I saw Aunt Ginger curling away from him; I saw the determined, uncompromising madness in Uncle Gerald's eyes and the terrible downward slant of his mouth.

"Sometimes I cannot rein in my temper," he said. "But I do not offer this as an excuse."

I found a perfect sand dollar, slid it into my pocket.

"I want to apologize to you, Master Trygve," he said, still facing the ocean and its roar.

"Okay," I said, but my small voice was blown back up the beach by the wind, and I knew he hadn't heard me. His voice had weight, for even though he had his back to me, I could hear him easily.

"I have already apologized to William," he said. "But I don't think he's accepted it. He can be a headstrong lad."

"He can," I agreed.

"I killed his mother, you know," he said.

I looked at his hands again. The thumbs seemed as big as the red rubber grips of bike handles. These were hands that could kill.

"Oh, not deliberately," he said. "It was my drinking. We were driving from Nanaimo to Ladysmith, over on Vancouver Island. William was a baby, asleep in the bassinet in the back seat. Philly—that was her name, short for Philomena—Philly and I had been drinking. It's an old story, Tryg. One you'll hear many more times before you get long in the tooth. Anyway, Philly said something that struck me wrong, and we had a fight. That perhaps doesn't surprise you. I reached for her and lost control of the car. We went off the road—not at high speed, mind you—and rammed a post. Philly flew out the door and broke her neck, simple as that. The car wasn't even damaged. I drove it away later. William slept through it. He went to sleep with a mother intact and woke up to no mother at all." He turned to me then and I was stunned to see that he'd been crying all the time he'd been talking to me. "Trygve, I can't tell you how sad life is. There are no bloody words for it."

I continued my hunt for shells. Uncle Gerald searched with me. We walked up the beach, not talking, staring at the sands. I found several more perfect sand dollars and a large piece of abalone shell. The rainbow hue of the shell's glossy interior seemed to me like the sky of a small and separate world.

"Well, well," Uncle Gerald said. "Look at this, Tryg."

He held up a clam. It was muddy and fat with contained life. Not pretty at all, completely uninteresting. But Uncle Gerald fanned the air with it before my eyes, insisting I pay attention to it. "This humble little chap might save your life someday, Tryg."

I looked at the shell again, then at Uncle Gerald.

"I see disbelief in your young face, lad," he said. He took a blunt mariner's knife from his pocket and pried open the shell. It took considerable effort, even for him, but he opened it perfectly. Then he scooped out the soft gray lump of flesh with the blade of his knife and popped it into his mouth. My automatic gag reflex lurched and I had to look away.

"Marvelous," Uncle Gerald said. "Bloody marvelous."

He dug into the wet sand with his blunt-nosed knife and found another clam, somewhat smaller than the first. "Now then, Tryg," he said. "Let's see what kind of sailor you are."

I watched, horrified, as he snapped open the shell and dug out the clam. He offered it to me on the blade of the knife, holding the clam fast under his big thumb.

"No thanks," I said, shaking my head.

He gave me a sidelong look, his eyes squinting with merry challenge. "Come on, be a manful bloke, Tryg. Take it."

My jaws were clamped together so tightly they ached. I shook my head.

"Look, Tryg. It's easy. You don't have to chew it. You couldn't chew it in fact. It just swims down your throat—nothing to it at all. It will make you grow an inch, it's so rich in food value."

He took my jaw in his hand gently. My mouth opened. He slid the clam off the knife and onto my tongue. It was not as big as I thought. Even so, my gag reflex would not allow it to swim down my throat. I held it in my mouth for a while, my eyes watering, a sandy drool slipping past my lips.

"That's it, lad. Just relax. Easy does it. Think of yourself as a stranded tar, no food for a week. Nothing between you and death by starvation but this lowly little mussel. It's all you've got, Tryg. You need it like you need the very air you breathe."

I saw myself starving on a beach, my wrecked Dauntless half submerged in the surf. A PBY rescue plane went over, looking for me, but I'd lost my signal mirror. I was slowly starving to death.

The clam went down. I shuddered, swallowed hard, swallowed again to stop my gorge from rising. Uncle Gerald clapped me on the back. "Good fellow!" he said. "Now, that wasn't so bad, was it? Just remember who taught you how to live for nothing on the beach, Tryg. Who knows, one day you might find yourself in dire circumstances."

Sick, but more proud than sick, I walked back up the beach where our blankets were spread.

↓

Malcolm, Betty, William, and I went to Santa Monica together on the Pacific Electric train. Directly overhead the sky was blue, but fog cut the horizon short. It was a chilly, windy day in late June. William and Betty went swimming anyway, while Malcolm and I stayed on the amusement pier. We spent most of our money on the airplanes. Side by side in a red biplane we tilted out over the breakers.

"Up your ass, Kraut," Malcolm said, squinting through the sights of his imaginary machine gun. He made the machine gun rattle, then the spitty explosion of the Stuka blowing up directly in front of us.

Malcolm fought his war over France, I fought mine out in the Pacific. My P-38 roared above the waves as I searched for my downed wingman, Wally Malone. A Mitsubishi dropped down on me from behind. I looked back at the airplane behind me, a blue monoplane with two junior high girls in it. "Shit!" I screamed at them. "Where the hell did *you* come from, Tokyo Joe?"

The junior high girls gave me the finger. I died sweetly in their arms.

The fog thickened. Malcolm and I walked down to the beach to see if we could find William and Betty. There were only a few swimmers braving the rough surf. We didn't see either one of them. Malcolm walked under the pier, up toward the sea wall. I followed him.

"I knocked down six Zeroes," I said, just to make conversation.

"Stukas," Malcolm said. "I got twenty of them."

"Twenty! Come on, twenty! Be realistic." I'd used one of Mitchell's favorite words. He liked to display his vocabulary and I always thought he was a show-off about it, but here I was doing the same thing. Another word he liked was "incredible." Another one was "basically." And so I now used both in a single sentence: "Malc, that's basically incredible."

Malcolm looked at me suspiciously. "What? For Chrissakes, Monk, talk English."

"You can't get twenty. No one ever gets twenty."

"I said twenty and I meant it, so what? I hate the Germans, Monk. Next time I'll get forty."

"But you've got to be germane," I said, using another of Mitchell's words.

"Huh? German? Did you say I've got to be a *German*?"

"No, *germane*," I said. I wasn't sure what it meant. "It means accurate," I said.

Malcolm grabbed my shoulder. "Don't ever call me German, Monk. I hate the fuckers."

"Is that because you're a Jew?" I asked. I was aware of Hitler's diatribe against the Jews and other races.

Malcolm gave me a long, careful look. "You're a genius, Monk," he said. "Hitler and the Nazis want to kill off the Jews. I'd like to kill *him*. Maybe someday I will."

"Even so," I said. "Knocking down twenty Stukas is basically—"

Malcolm farted.

"Gone with the wind," I said.

We walked for a while without speaking, kicking at clumps of seaweed, picking up a nice shell here and there. Ahead of us on the sea wall someone had drawn a "Kilroy Was Here" figure. You saw them everywhere, scrawled on the sides of buildings, on fences, on sidewalks, on the dusty windows of parked cars. The drawn figure of Kilroy fascinated me. He was always the same, no matter who drew him—an essentially faceless character who peeked out at the world from behind a fence, just his eyes and sometimes his hands showing. Like this:

Who was Kilroy? Why had he been here? "Here," of course, meant everywhere since that's where you saw Kilroy—everywhere. I thought about this as we sauntered up toward the dark end of the underside of the Santa Monica pier. Kilroy was here. *Was.* That was the germane word—*was.* Kilroy *was* here meant he *no longer* was here. He was now elsewhere. Yet he peered out at you from the sides of buildings, from parked cars, and from the sea wall at Santa Monica.

Kilroy was here. But now he was gone. Like the billions and billions of dead. Faceless, without identity, everywhere. Like the ghost of collective humanity itself.

Or like a vampire.

It made sense. Kilroy, like the vampire in the Bela Lugosi movies, was the thing that survived after its victim had been bled dry. The live-dead thing that went on and on throughout eternity.

"Kilroy the vampire was here," I said.

"Crazy Monk," Malcolm said.

"No, really," I said. "See, if—"

"Monk, I'm going to take a piss. Let me take a piss without you talking about vampires and stuff, okay?"

I took a piss, too. Side by side we arced yellow ribbons into the dark sand. "You're different," I said.

"*You're* different," he said.

"I mean your pecker," I said.

Side by side, we compared our parallel peckers.

"Your pecker looks weird," I said.

"Yours is the weird pecker, Monk," he said.

"You don't have anything on it," I said.

"Foreskin you mean," he said. "No, I'm circumcised. That stupid flap of skin on the end of yours is called the foreskin."

"Circumcised? You mean they cut the foreskin *off?*"

"They do it when you're a baby. That way it doesn't kill you. It's a Jewish thing."

We stood there looking at our dissimilar peckers. So that's what being Jewish meant. Hitler wanted to kill off the Jews because of their dissimilar peckers.

"What are you two queers up to?" William said.

He and Betty had followed us. I stuffed my pecker back into my blue jeans and buttoned up. Malcolm did the same. We kept our backs to William and Betty.

"I told you that cousin of yours was creepy," Betty said.

"He's no cousin of mine," William said. "He's Dracula's cousin, as far as I can make out."

"That's basically incredible, William," I said, mustering all the dignity I could. I walked away from them, gliding on the balls of my feet, graceful, smooth, and sophisticated.

The four of us walked up Ocean Park Boulevard to the Douglas plant. Several blocks before we reached the plant, we found ourselves under a huge net. It was a camouflage net, spanning the boulevard, rising to a peak above the main Douglas factory, sloping down to the far side of it, and festooned with cardboard scenery, which, when seen from high above by the crew of a bomber, looked like ordinary farmland. Looking up from the street, we could see houses, barns, herds of dairy cows, trees, and the various colors of the countryside. It was like being buried hundreds of feet in the earth but having the power of X-ray vision, like Superman, so that we could see all the way to the surface.

"The Japs won't fall for it," William said, spitting.

"Why not?" I asked. It seemed like a great idea to me—the entire industrial area concealed from the air by being made to look like a rural scene.

"For one thing, look where we are. California. What they've got hooked on to that net is what you'd see in the Midwest. Look, they don't even have a palm tree up there. I think the Japs would take one look at that and laugh their asses off. The nut who designed it must have been from Iowa."

I was offended. "Yeah, but the Japs wouldn't know about *that*," I said.

"Do you think they're *stupid*, Monk?" William said. "Do you think someone who could take over most of the Pacific Ocean is stupid?"

I'd never thought about the Japanese as having brains. They were just murderous *Japs* who didn't care about their own lives. But if they had *brains,* that made them more frightening than ever. What if they were as smart as Americans? What if William was right and the Jap pilots who reached Los Angeles just laughed at the camouflage nets over Douglas and other defense plants? For the first time, it actually occurred to me that we might *not* win the war.

"Don't worry about it, Monk," Malcolm said. "They don't have any long-range bombers like the B-17 or B-24."

William spit with artistic skill between Malcolm's feet. "How do you know that, Malc?" he said.

"Because I'm an air spotter. I've got a chart that shows all the Jap planes. Their best bomber can only fly about twenty-six hundred miles."

"If they take off from carriers that might be enough," William said.

"The Betty can't take off from carriers," Malcolm said.

Betty, who had not said much on our walk, perked up at the mention of her name. "They named a bomber after me?" she said, fluttering her eyelashes. "Why, I'm *flattered*."

Malcolm scratched his head. "Well, if they used carriers, they'd probably hit us with the Judy. It's got a range of about thirteen hundred miles."

"It could happen," William said.

"No it couldn't!" I shouted, surprising myself. "It couldn't happen!" I ran up the street from them, pursued, in my chaotic imagination, by Sylvester Snell in a Japanese uniform, carrying a rifle with a long bayonet.

"You're mine," he said.

☙

Now that Uncle Gerald was home, the small apartment seemed twice as small. Uncle Gerald and Aunt Ginger occupied the front room, sleeping in the Murphy bed. Aunt Ginger slept there when Uncle Gerald was out to sea, but she didn't "occupy" it. Every morning before anyone else got up, Aunt Ginger would have the bed made and folded back into the wall. I'd usually find her sitting in the kitchen with her cup of coffee, listening to the table model radio. But with Uncle Gerald home, the front room was always littered with wrinkled clothes, newspapers, ashtrays full of butts and cigarette wrappers. Uncle Gerald liked to sleep in when he was on shore leave and so the front room was generally off-limits until about 10 A.M. And since we had to walk through the front room to get to the kitchen, William and I were more or less confined to our small bedroom. I liked our bedroom, but I hated confinement.

Our bedroom was situated between the front room and Mitchell's and Mother's bedroom. At night I could hear arguing voices through the walls. Through one wall the voices of Mitchell and Mother ground on through the night. I could make out most of what was said. Mitchell wanted Aunt Ginger to get her own apartment so that Uncle Gerald would have a place to go when his ship was in. Mitchell didn't care for Uncle Gerald very much and wanted him out, but Mother felt obligated to take care of her younger sister. "She's not doing well," I heard Mother say. "She may get canned." And Mitchell replied, "There are limits to obligation, dear. Be realistic. Are you going to protect her all your life?" "If I have to," Mother said. "That's incredible," Mitchell said. "Utterly incredible."

From the other wall it was mostly Uncle Gerald's heavy voice that I heard. Aunt Ginger didn't really argue with him, she just provided a kind of weak, unintelligible response to his constant harangues. Now and then she would break into sobs, but this only increased the violence of Uncle Gerald's verbal assault.

The nightly arguments, the sense of cramped quarters with too many people breathing up the apartment's air, and the heat wave that had descended on Los Angeles made me claustrophobic. I looked for escape by listening to my shortwave radio, but the tangle of foreign voices and Morse code became part of my claustrophobia too. I wanted to go out to the kitchen and sit at the table. I wanted to pour myself a cold glass of milk and thumb through magazines, but I would have to intrude on Uncle Gerald's grinding attacks on Aunt Ginger, and I didn't have the nerve to do this.

So I lay sweating in bed next to William, who had become a chain-smoker. He would light up in the middle of the night and smoke three or four cigarettes before going back to sleep. This worried me. What if he dropped a cigarette on the covers and a deadly fire started? This concern added to my trapped feeling.

On Uncle Gerald's last night of shore leave, the temperature must have been in the nineties. No breeze moved the curtains in the wide-open window. They hung limp in the unusually humid air. I slept only for a few minutes at a time, and when I did sleep I had dreams that were more like memories than dreams. In one dream I stood under the camouflage net covering the Douglas plant watching Jap bombers of the "Judy" class release bomb after bomb. The bombs were caught in the net and, like circus high-wire performers, were trampolined back into the sky. The big net shook with the impact of the endlessly bouncing bombs. When one came to rest above my head, I could hear it tinkling. Piano music was coming from it.

I woke up. William was smoking a cigarette and staring at the ceiling. He looked dusty gray in the smoky glow of a distant streetlight. I kicked the covers off my side of the bed and propped myself up on one elbow. "Listen to that," William said. I heard Mitchell laughing scornfully on the intake of breath, muted behind the wall but still potent enough to grate my nerves.

"He sounds like a jackass," I said.

"Not him," William said. "The music. It's her. She's playing."

"Who?" I said. "Who's playing?" Mitchell stopped laughing and I heard Betty's piano. She was playing classical music, Chopin or Debussy—the two composers she talked about most often.

"She's damned good," William said.

"Maybe she'll play in the Hollywood Bowl someday," I said.

"Could be," William said.

"I don't see what's so funny," I heard Mother say.

"She's nuts," Mitchell said. "That's what's so funny. She's nuts and you expect me to take her seriously."

"She isn't *nuts*," Mother said. "She's different. We have to understand her."

"They'll understand her a lot better up in Napa," he said.

"Where's Napa?" I asked.

"Up north," William said. "North of Frisco. There's a nut-house up there. They'll probably send you there someday, Monk."

He sucked on his cigarette, making it crackle.

"Hell if they will," I said.

William laughed. "It won't be so bad, Monk. You'll like it. You can talk about vampires and shit, and whatever else, and no one will mind."

"I don't see why you're so dead set against her," Mother said.

"I'm not dead set against anybody," Mitchell said. "I just want you to be realistic. Ginger's got to straighten up and fly right. When Gerald leaves, I want you to get her to a psychiatrist."

"She's not insane!" Mother said.

"Jesus Christ," William said, lighting a fresh cigarette. "I'm clearing out."

"You said that a long time ago," I said.

"If I said it, then I meant it," he said.

The piano music rose to a peak, filling the room like a strong breeze. "I'll go when the time is right, Monk, and not before," he said.

"I didn't say she was insane," Mitchell said.

"You said she was nuts," Mother said. "What did you mean if you didn't mean she was insane?"

"She's not insane *yet,* is what I meant," Mitchell said. "But if she keeps acting as she does, then, realistically speaking, it's obvious that she's heading in that direction."

"I don't think you care at all about where she's headed," Mother said. "I think you're worrying about your phony movie friend."

Mitchell laughed. "Phony? I'm going to meet Franchot Tone. What's phony about that?"

"I'll believe it when I see it," Mother said.

"You'll see it. And I don't want Ginger mooning around here when Jack brings Mr. Tone over."

"So that's it!" Mother said. "I should have known. You're afraid Ginger will embarrass you in front of the great Franchot Tone!"

"I have to think about my career," Mitchell said. "It's *your* future, too, you know."

"Jesus Christ!" Mother and William said together.

William got out of bed and stepped through the window. I followed him. We walked out into the vacant lot in our pajamas.

"I think we *live* in a nuthouse, Monk," William said.

We went into the fort where William lit up another cigarette.

↓

To become an air spotter you had to send in the top of a cereal box along with a dollar bill to someplace in Ohio, and in return you received a chart that displayed the side-view and bottom-view silhouettes of both Japanese and German warplanes. You also got a pair of tin binoculars. Your assignment, according to the written instructions that accompanied the air spotter's kit, was to observe the sky as long as possible each day. If you spotted the silhouette of an enemy aircraft, you were to report it immediately to the nearest military authority, noting the intruder's compass direction and its estimated speed and altitude. I sent in my box top and dollar and two weeks later received my kit. Malcolm and I spent days that summer lying on our backs on the roof of the apartment building searching the skies above Los Angeles with our tin binoculars. We looked for Bettys, Judys, Tonys, Helens, Irvings, and Nicks, manufactured by Mitsubishi, Kawasaki, Nakajima, and Yokosuka. The American names were given to these warplanes by the military, who needed a quick and memorable way of identifying them. Several times I thought I spotted Zeroes. My heart jumped in my chest every time I thought a Zero crossed my field of vision. But they were only American A T-6s, a training plane used by both the army and navy. Zeroes and A T-6s had similar silhouettes. It was believed that the Mitsubishi company had copied the A T-6 when they designed the Zero. Of course the Zero was a high-speed, short-range interceptor and there was little chance that it would be attacking Los Angeles as it had Pearl Harbor. But you could never be sure.

The skies over Los Angeles were crowded with airplanes that summer. The drone and whine were constant. Test pilots from all the major aircraft plants put their planes through the paces straight over our heads. P-38s dove and twisted through the stratosphere. Douglas Dauntless S B D s moaned at low level skipping imaginary bombs through the hot streets. Huge formations of B-25 Mitchells shook the buildings. Sleek P-51 Mustangs had dogfights with one another at altitudes so rarefied they could only be seen through the binoculars. The high-flying B-24s left vapor trails as they crossed from west to east on their way to England.

I stationed myself on one end of the roof, Malcolm on the other. We communicated by means of battery-operated telegraph sets. We were both learning Morse code and could tap out our names, as well as most aircraft designations, intelligibly. The sets were connected to each other by wire and messages sent on one set would make a buzzer sound on the other. If there was danger of enemy agents overhearing the buzzer, it could be switched off and a small bulb would light up with the dots and dashes of Morse code.

Sometimes boredom would get the better of us. I'd give up the skies and scan the street below with my binoculars. Once I saw William and Betty walking up Ridgely from Adams Boulevard. They were holding hands. I called Malcolm over and we both observed them. They had just been to a matinee at the Variety to see *Casablanca*. William was smoking a cigarette. I noticed, even from two blocks away, that he was inhaling.

"Lovers," Malcolm said.

William and Betty stopped by a lamppost. Betty leaned her back against it and William lit a cigarette for her. They both inhaled.

"I can read their lips," Malcolm said.

I adjusted my binoculars, but I couldn't see any lip movement.

"William just said, 'Betty, you've got an enormous set of headlights.'"

I looked at Malcolm. "Baloney," I said.

"'How about I take a look at those headlights, Betty,' William just said."

"You're full of it," I said.

"They're kissing," Malcolm said.

"Come off it," I said, but when I turned my binoculars back on them I saw it was true. Right out in broad daylight, their cigarettes held carefully out to one side so that they wouldn't accidently burn each other, they kissed. It was a long, busy kiss.

"Holy cow," I said.

"They think they're Humphrey Bogart and Ingrid Bergman," Malcolm said.

In the binoculars, I could see William squinting like Bogart, a wry, Bogart-like smile on his face.

"Two bits he gets her cherry," Malcolm said.

I knew approximately what he meant. "The hell," I said. "They're too young."

Malcolm lowered his binoculars and looked at me. He gave me a deadpan stare, then winked. "Monk, you kill me. You're a rare one, Monk."

We both laughed like ruined men of the world.

I took credit for having made a joke, even though I didn't get it.

↓

The Bruckners didn't have blackout curtains, so when a blackout was called they had to turn out their lights. The four of us—Malcolm, Betty, William, and I—were playing Parcheesi on the kitchen table when the sirens sounded. Malcolm got up and turned out all the lights. Across Los Angeles the sirens wailed. It was thrilling, like the end of the world was being signaled.

The Bruckners' apartment was on the third floor, the top floor of the apartment building, and from the kitchen window we could see the long arms of searchlights reach across the sky. Now and then a cloud would flare as a beam caught it. It was better than a Fourth of July fireworks display since it was tense with the possibility of mortal danger. A year earlier, the searchlights trapped what they thought was a Japanese plane. Anti-aircraft batteries lit up the sky with ack-ack and tracer rounds. Many of the rounds didn't explode until they came back to earth, killing several citizens and starting fires. I hoped for something like that to happen again. I wanted to live through an air attack, I wanted to see a plane trapped in the crossed beams of a dozen searchlights as the anti-aircraft guns poured tracers into it.

William lit up a cigarette and handed it to Betty. Then he lit one for himself.

"Those matches can be seen ten miles away," I said.

"We're goners then," William said. "The Japs have our number now. I just hope it's short and sweet, right between the eyes."

"I'm serious," I said.

"When aren't you, Monk?" Malcolm said.

I went into the front room and turned on the Bruckners' Zenith, switching it to shortwave.

"Watch it, Monk," William said. "The Japs can see that radio dial a hundred miles out to sea. What are you trying to do, give them the position of Los Angeles? You some kind of spy, Monk?"

"Shut up," I said, trying to find Australia.

"You could be hung as a traitor, Monk," William said. "I personally don't think you're a traitor, but who's to say the F B I won't?"

"Maybe we should put him in the closet for his own protection," Betty said. "That way he won't be able to give the Japs any secret information about where Los Angeles is."

The thought of Betty Bruckner putting me into a closet sent an illicit chill through me. I knew, the instant she said it, that I'd construct elaborate fantasies around that notion for days.

Naked and glistening from her shower, she'd pull me by the hand to her closet. My reluctance would be undermined by this same exciting illicit chill. In the closet she'd push me down among her shoes. I could almost smell the leather of her shoes, the intimate foot-smell of them, and the pressing claustrophobic air of the closet. "You stay here," she'd say, "until the Gestapo have left. They won't think to search for you in here." And before she left me lying alone in the closet among her fragrant shoes, she'd say, "I'm so proud of you for what you have done for my people. You are the bravest man I've ever known." I would shrug. Her breasts, caught in the sudden beam of a searchlight, would shine.

William and Betty came into the front room and sat on the sofa. Between stations, in the deadspots on the dial, I could hear Betty go, "Umm, umm," and the wet sound of lips sliding together and coming apart and the rush of humid breath. I switched off the radio and went back into the kitchen.

"Monk, look," Malcolm said. He pointed out the window into a bright matrix of searchlights. Like a fly in a spider's web, a tiny plane was caught in the beams. "Geez-O!" he said. "I bet that guy is pissing his pants."

"Maybe it's a Jap," I said.

"Either way, I bet he's pissing all over himself."

I waited urgently for the ack-ack guns, but they didn't fire.

↓

Garland Quince—Franchot Tone's agent, according to Jack Twilly at least—came to dinner. He was a diminutive man with black hair that looked lacquered. He wore a waxed mustache that was wide as a toothpick. There was a toy poodle tucked under his arm. The poodle's lip was drawn up, showing small hostile teeth.

"Mr. Tone can't do anything for you," Jack Twilly said to Mitchell. "I mean, he's an *actor*, a big star to be sure, but he's not interested in lining up a screen test for you. The man for that job is Garland here. He's got the best nose for talent in this burg."

Mitchell looked dubious at first, then, as he shook Garland Quince's small hand, he perked up. "I'm a great admirer of Mr. Tone's work," Mitchell said.

Garland Quince regarded Mitchell with a bored, uninterested gaze. "When do we eat?" he said.

Jack Twilly laughed nervously. "How about we have a drink first, Mitch?" he said.

Garland Quince looked at his wristwatch. "I must yet to see Mr. de Mille this evening," he said. His accent could have been French, Spanish, or Russian—I couldn't place it, and I'd been listening to the voices of all nations for months on my shortwave radio.

Mitchell made some highballs and brought them into the front room on a tray. Garland Quince took a glass and sniffed it. "I must tell you, Meetch," he said. "I do not take on the new-coming greenhorn without first a fee. The greenhorn has not proved nothing to nobody yet. If I take on a nobody then the gamble is for me alone, you see? So I ask the fee, in this case, of the nobody."

"Fee?" Mitchell said.

"One hundred dollars," Garland Quince said, sipping his drink.

"Because the gamble is all his, Mitch," Jack Twilly said. "He's going to make phone calls on your behalf, he's going to twist arms—all of this *costs*."

Garland Quince put his toy poodle on the sofa. "Stay put, Hermione," he said. The poodle curled up on the sofa obediently, but raised its head to sniff at the aroma that was coming from the kitchen. Mother had baked a ham and was now tossing the salad.

"A *hundred*," Mitchell said, scratching his head. "I don't know..."

"You said he was serious for his career," Garland Quince said to Jack Twilly.

"Franchot Tone gets a hundred thousand per picture, Mitch," Jack Twilly said. "You're going to balk at a measly hundred when the stakes are that high? Maybe there's something you don't understand, Mitch. Just *getting* an agent like Garland here is three-quarters of the battle. Am I right or wrong, Garland?"

Garland Quince didn't answer. He slid an ebony cigarette holder out of his breast pocket and fitted a Chesterfield into it. Jack Twilly lit it for him.

I had been setting the table, and now Mother brought in the big glazed ham. Six of us were eating dinner that night. William had taken Betty out to a ball game—the Hollywood Stars were playing the Sacramento Solons out at Gilmore Field. Neither William nor Betty was interested in Pacific Coast League baseball, they just wanted an excuse to be together.

"Dinner is served," Mitchell said.

"And who is *this*—Sonja Heine?" Garland Quince said, bowing elegantly to Mother.

Mother didn't acknowledge the compliment.

"Sonja Heine, my wife," Mitchell said—then laughed. The great throat-wrenching rasp shook the air.

"When Sonja was my client," Garland Quince said, "she taught to me the figure eight."

"Sonja Heine was your client, too?" Mitchell said.

"Yes, yes," Garland Quince said, laughing bitterly. "I made her the star, then she deserted me—but that is a very old story, my friend. You will hear it many times before long if you are to involve yourself with this business."

Involving himself in that business was exactly what Mitchell wanted. Hearing himself included among those insiders who knew about betrayals and trachery made him beam with pleasure.

"You've got to read the fine print twice," Mitchell said, adopting Garland Quince's sophisticated view of the movie business.

I saw Jack Twilly and Garland Quince exchange brief, deadpan glances.

"My God!" Garland Quince said. "Look at this *ham*. Mrs. Selfage, how did you manage to procure such a fine ham?"

Mitchell winked at Jack Twilly.

"He's a milkman, Garland," Jack Twilly said. "He's got gas stamps, too."

"Ah," Garland Quince said, drawing out the syllable. "Very excellent. Very excellent, in*deed*."

I saw the two movie men exchange glances again. Mitchell saw only the klieg lights of his future.

"Trygve," Mother said. "Go see if Ginger is going to come out or not."

Aunt Ginger was in my bedroom, sitting at the small desk, reading a novel. "Tell her I'm not eating," she said. "Tell her I'll snack later. I don't feel like being with those men tonight."

She'd been in my room most of the day, reading her novels. She hadn't eaten lunch and had had only a slice of toast for breakfast. It was Sunday, and we usually ate heavily on Sundays.

"I'll tell her you feel sick," I said.

"Tell her I'm sick, Trygve. That's right. Tell her I'm not feeling well." She looked up from her book and smiled at me. Her smile was sad and angelic, like the smile of a condemned person forgiving the executioner.

"Okay," I said, and turned to leave.

"Wait," she said. "I want you to listen to something." She picked up her novel and opened it to the last page. It was *The Bridge of San Luis Rey,* a book that she'd read several times since we'd all been living together. "'There is a land of the living and a land of the dead and the bridge is love,'" she read. "'The only survival, the only meaning.'"

She looked at me again and I looked away, shy with ignorance.

"I know you don't understand it yet," she said gently, "but I want you to remember it because someday, all of a sudden, you *will* understand it. And when that moment comes, you are going to need it, Trygve. You are going to need it badly, the way a person dying of thirst needs water."

"I'll tell Mother you're sick," I mumbled.

"'Life is too fearful to bear,'" she said, quoting from her novel again. "'When may I die?'"

"I'll tell her you're *real* sick," I said, finding purpose in my role of providing a buffer between my sick aunt and the heartless world. That, after all, was what the soldiers, sailors, and airmen *did,* wasn't it? They sacrificed themselves to the cruelties that raged across the oceans, for the sake of all the helpless civilians.

But when I went back out to the dinner table everyone had already begun to eat, Aunt Ginger or no Aunt Ginger. I took my seat and helped myself to a thick slice of black market ham, a scoop of scalloped potatoes, plump peas with pearl onions mixed in, and a Parker House roll dripping authentic yellow butter.

☟

The sky above the Rhineland was salmon pink. The drone of the four engines of my B-24 lulled me into a sense of peaceful admiration for the beauty of the German morning. Tyrone North, my co-pilot, yelled, too late, "Duck, Charlie!" The sky was suddenly thick with black carnations. We flew straight into them. One bloomed into the windshield of the B-24, breaking it. I didn't feel anything. Then a warm wetness spread over my face. "It missed my eyes, Ty," I said.

I woke up to soaked pillows and sheets. My nose had started bleeding in my sleep. I got up and went into the bathroom and saw that my pajama top was soaked with blood. I washed my face with cold water and pinched the bleeding nostril shut, but the blood just backed up and came out the other nostril. When I pinched both sides of my nose shut, the blood rushed down my throat.

"What happened to you, Trygve?" Mother asked.

She was in the doorway to the bathroom, her arms folded against her breasts. She was in her bathrobe and there was a clear gel on her face.

"I don't know," I said. "I woke up and my nose was bleeding."

She washed my face off and tried to hold my nostrils shut, but the blood kept coming. Then she went into the kitchen and came back with a tray full of ice cubes. She wrapped the ice cubes in a washcloth and pressed it to the back of my neck. I was leaning over the sink, watching the blood drip onto the porcelain and slide down toward the drain. The ice pack on the back of my neck seemed to slow the drips, but it didn't stop them. After about a half hour of this, I began to get scared.

"I think I've lost a lot of blood," I said.

"Yes," my mother said, "you have."

I began to cry. I choked back the sobs to make it sound as if I were only clearing blood out of my throat. Mother pulled me away from the sink. She sat on the toilet seat and made me sit in her lap. I leaned my head on her shoulder. She hummed an old Norwegian lullaby. I didn't understand any Norwegian, but I liked the sound of it. It made me relaxed and dreamy. I held the cold washcloth to my nose, but it was only a gesture. The blood rolled down and soon we were both covered with it. It fell down between Mother's bare feet, splattering them. It pooled on the small white tiles of the bathroom floor.

Mitchell came in, looking for Mother. "What happened?" he said, his face white.

"Nosebleeds run in our family," Mother said. "My brothers got them all the time when they were kids."

"Jesus," Mitchell said. "This is worse than a nosebleed. He's hemorrhaging."

I swallowed a mouthful of the raw-tasting, salty flood. I tried to smile bravely, knowing my teeth were red. Mitchell's eyes rolled upward and he fell. He fell hard, like he'd been shot. His head slammed the wall—deliberately, it seemed—and I thought he'd gone crazy. But then he hit the floor with the natural velocity of dead weight in free fall. He lay there, unmoving.

"What's wrong with Mitchell?" I said.

"He fainted. He hates the sight of blood," Mother said.

"Aren't you going to help him?" I said.

"He'll be all right, Trygve," she said, stroking my hair. "I'm more concerned about you right now."

Mitchell groaned and pushed himself up to a sitting position. He saw his blood-soaked family sitting on the toilet and turned his head away. "You can't stop it, can you?" he said, facing the door.

"No, I don't think so," Mother said.

"I'll get the car out," he said. "We'd better take him to the hospital."

"I'll be okay," I said.

"You're *not* okay," Mitchell said.

Actually, I felt dizzy. Now and then a black spot the size of a dime would float across my field of vision. The first time I saw it I thought it was a spider and moved my hand to brush it away.

Mitchell got to his feet and left the bathroom.

"Don't worry, Tryg," Mother said. "They can stop it at the hospital. It isn't fatal. Your uncles had them all the time until they were in their late teens."

"I don't want to go to the hospital," I said.

"Luckily, your vote doesn't count," she said.

The hospital, like the foster home, or my grandparents' house, meant separation again. There was no guarantee that the world would be intact when I got out. Everything might change drastically if I weren't there to keep an eye on it.

"I'll be fine," I said, watching a pair of black dimes bump together playfully.

"Yes, you will," Mother said. "That's what hospitals are for."

Mitchell woke up William. He'd slept through my nosebleed and was astonished to find himself soaked in blood. I heard William cursing as he got dressed.

"I'm going to start the car," Mitchell said, coming back into the bathroom, head averted. "William will help you get Tryg ready."

Mother left me on the toilet seat holding the washcloth against my face while she got dressed. She put on her work clothes, planning, I guessed, to stay with me at the hospital until it was time for her to go on shift. William came in.

"What's with you, Monk?" he said, running a comb through the tap water and then through his hair. "You trying to paint the house red?"

His joke made me feel better. I swallowed another salty mouthful and smiled. "Sure," I said, feeling heroic. "I like red."

Mitchell covered the back seat of the Cadillac with a wool blanket so that my blood wouldn't stain the upholstery. I sat between

Mother and William, holding my nose shut, swallowing my blood until I started to feel sick. To relieve my sick stomach, I'd let the blood run out of my nose for a while, catching it in a towel.

When we reached Los Angeles General Hospital, it was almost dawn. By this time I'd lost enough blood to feel lightheaded. William carried me up the endless front steps of the huge, dark building. I was in a dreamy mood. The sky above me widened suddenly as the black clouds separated and dispersed. The light, expanding in the gulf left by the opening clouds, was salmon pink—just as it had been in my war dream.

"Ty," I mumbled. "I've been hit."

"What?" William said.

"I'm cold," I said.

"You'll be warm in a minute," William said. His tone of voice was different. Usually he used a joking and sometimes an impatient or mocking tone with me. Now he seemed unsure of himself—even kindly.

Mother held the door open while William carried me inside. Mitchell stayed in the double-parked car. An elderly nurse, noticing that I was spattering the white tiled floor of the waiting room with blood, waved us down the hall to a small, brightly lit examination room. "The doctor's on his way," she said.

When the doctor arrived, Mother and William were asked to leave. Mother kissed my forehead and William gave me a little sock on the jaw. "Keep your chin up, Monk," he said.

I tried to smile at him but my lips were stuck together with congealed blood.

"Looks like something opened your spigot, young man," the doctor said.

A nurse helped me up to a tall examination table, then she had me lie on my back. Fresh blood salted my throat and my stomach got queasy again. The doctor pulled a bright light down close to my face and looked up my nose with an instrument.

"We'll pack it," he said to the nurse.

The nurse went to a cabinet and returned with a red rubber tube. The doctor took the tube from her and leaned down to me.

"This will be a little uncomfortable, but we'll get it over within a minute if you cooperate. Just lie very still, okay"—he picked up a sheet of paper and squinted at it—"okay, Trygve?"

I nodded. He slid the tube into my right nostril. When it reached the back of my nose it began to hurt. Tears filled my eyes and I wanted to sneeze. He kept pushing the tube in. I couldn't believe it—it seemed he wanted it to go up into my brain. I grabbed his wrist. "Onk onk," I said.

"Relax, Trygve. It'll just take another second," he said.

He reached into my mouth and pulled the end of the tube out. A string inside the tube was connected to the pack—a cylinder of gauze thick as a finger. The doctor continued to pull the rubber tube out of my nose through my mouth, leaving the pack of gauze in its place. To imbed the pack in my nostril, he pulled on the string dangling at the back of my throat. I gagged violently but he ignored me and tied the two ends of the string at my lip. He stepped back, pleased with a job well done.

"We'll keep that in for a few days, Trygve," he said. "By then the bleeding should have stopped."

"Onk," I said, immediately regretting it. The string at the back of my nose sawed against my soft palate when I spoke. Even swallowing hurt. I wasn't hungry at all, but the thought occurred to me: How was I going to eat?

The nurse was a large woman who seemed swollen. Her swollen breasts strained against the front of her dress causing the buttons to pull mightily against the threads holding them. She had a large swollen neck. Her face was round as a pie and pink. Looking at her clean, pink flesh made me think of food. Food in the oven, cakes and cookies and roasts. She reminded me of soap, too. Big pink bars of Lifebuoy with its strong, astringent smell. She leaned down to me and gently washed the crusty blood from my lips with a warm washcloth. "We're going to take such good care of you, Trygve," she said, "that you're not going to want to go home, ever."

↓

I was taken to the children's ward and put to bed between a boy in a body cast and a girl with blue and yellow splotches all over her arms and neck. They were both sleeping. The swollen nurse turned me over gently and pulled my pajama bottoms down. "This will sting a bit," she said, injecting me with penicillin. The needle didn't hurt but the penicillin felt like fire as it entered me. "You're going to get a lot of these, Trygve," she said. "One every three hours for a day or two."

"Onk," I said, forgetting my vow of silence.

"Doctor's orders. He thinks you've got a real bad infection in your nose. That's why it started bleeding like that."

She pulled my pajamas up and turned me over. She tucked me into the clean white bedding. "I'm Mrs. Silver," she said. Her name made me smile and the smile stretched the string on my lips. The tightened string sawed at my soft palate and tears leaked out of my eyes. I smiled because the only other Silver I knew was the Lone Ranger's horse. It amused me to think that the Lone Ranger's horse had a human wife who worked in Los Angeles General Hospital as a nurse.

I went to sleep that morning thinking about radio and movie horses and their human wives—Mrs. Trigger, Mrs. Tony, Mrs. Scout, Mrs. Thunder—all working as nurses in Los Angeles General. I was awakened three hours later out of a war dream—I was lying wounded in an English hospital with horses gathered around my bed—to get my second shot of penicillin. A new nurse gave me the shot, a young, pretty woman who sang continually. "Love me or leave me and let me be lonely," she sang in a pretty alto voice. Even when her eyes met mine she didn't stop singing.

"She thinks she's Helen O'Connell," said the boy in the body cast, after the nurse left the ward.

I couldn't see much of him, just part of his nose as it poked above the surrounding plaster, but judging from the pitch of his voice, I put his age at around fifteen.

"Ohnz," I said, as softly as possible, just to let him know that I'd heard and understood him, and to make him realize that I wasn't going to be able to hold conversations with him.

"She's okay, though," he said. "Especially when bath time comes around. You're going to like bath time, she's crazy about giving baths to the boys."

This worried me a bit. I was at the age where privacy was a necessity. I didn't like to let my mother into the bathroom when I was taking a bath or sitting on the toilet. Sometimes she'd barge in anyway, when she was in a hurry, and it always made me resentful. I wasn't exactly embarrassed, I just felt that my rights as an individual were not being recognized. The notion of a total stranger giving me a bath, though, was a definite escalation of the problem. A cheering thought occurred to me: I probably wouldn't be here long enough to need a bath. Three or four days at most, and how could I possibly get dirty in that time just lying in bed?

"Every day, about six o'clock, right after dinner," the boy next to me said, as if reading my thoughts. "Whether you need it or not."

I realized then that he had to be lying. He was covered with plaster, head to toe. There was no way he could be getting baths from that nurse. What was there to *bathe?* I noticed two other boys across the ward leaning on their elbows to get a good look at me. They were smiling, enjoying the joke the boy in the body cast was playing.

By late afternoon my buttocks began to tighten automatically at the sight of the nurse with her syringe tray. I ached from all the shots and dreaded the fiery penicillin. But I was feeling better. My queasiness had gone and I actually felt hungry. Lunch had been a cup of consommé and a glass of orange juice. I wanted meat and potatoes now, but knew I could not have swallowed anything with substance. When supper came—more consommé and juice—I gulped it down and asked for seconds.

I felt good and wanted to go home. I whispered this to the singing nurse, but she only smiled and told me to be patient. She pulled a screen around my bed, creating a private cubicle. Then she pulled off my covers and loosened the drawstrings of my pajama bottoms. "It's time for your evening bath, Trygve," she said, in her lovely, singsong voice. She pulled my pajama bottoms off and then slid my arms out of the tops. Through an opening in the screen she pulled in a wheeled cart with bathing equipment on it: a large pan of warm water, a sponge, a washcloth, cotton swabs, and a towel.

It killed me to do it, but I managed to say, "I don't need a bath, ma'am." My articulation was minimal and she stared at me for a few seconds, deciphering.

"Oh, yes. Baths are required. This is a hospital, Trygve. We aren't allowed to keep unclean patients. After all, we give you clean sheets every day, don't we? Why should we do that for filthy patients?"

I lapsed into weak onks. "Onk onk onk," I said, meaning, "I don't know."

She understood me, though. Not my words but my acquiescence. I relaxed back into my pillow and stared at the white ceiling. She began to sing again as she dipped the washcloth into the pan of warm water. "When the lights go on again, all over the world," she sang, her voice plaintive and sad. Her melancholy tone made me think that she had a boyfriend or husband overseas. I imagined him an airman, a fighter pilot stationed in London. He flew P-51 Mustangs and had shot down twelve Messerschmitt M E-109s before getting shot down himself. He was lying, legless, in a hospital on the outskirts of London. He couldn't remember his name or where he came from, and no one had told him yet that his legs had been amputated. He could remember his girlfriend or wife, but only her pretty face and mournful singing voice, not her name. "Jenny," he'd cry out in his delirium. Then he'd sink back into his confused gloom. "No, not Jenny," he'd mumble.

The nurse started with my feet. She passed the washcloth between my toes, sawing it back and forth slightly. The back-and-forth motion of the washcloth sent wave after wave of chills up my legs and back. When she reached my knees she interrupted her song. "Ugh," she said. She shook her head at the impossible task of dealing with my knees. My knees were coarse with ground-in dirt. "Elephant skin," she said. She rubbed Ivory soap into the thickened skin, hoping to soften it. Frustrated, she traded the washcloth for a soft-bristled brush. "Boys," she said, compressing her lips. The action of the bristles stirred me in a way I hadn't been stirred before. My inner thighs began to sweat.

She gave up on my knees and moved to my sweating thighs. My stomach growled and my heart began to beat noticeably. I was afraid she could see it banging against my chest bones. I let my hand fall nonchalantly over my thumping heart. The washcloth moved up my inner thighs to my crotch. I gritted my teeth against a howl that was rising from my innards. She slid the warm washcloth with great care and gentleness under my privates and then around them. My face, I was sure, could ignite paper. I glanced at the three black hairs on the back of my hand, fighting back a Lon Chaney wolfman yelp. She pushed the careful washcloth to my anus. I stiffened as if a thousand volts of alternating current had passed through me.

She seized my nodding penis. She made no comment on its aggravated state. I closed my eyes and imagined flaming death over Germany. It didn't help. "Oh *dear*," she said, her voice low with disappointment. My heart hesitated. I opened my eyes cautiously. With the extreme care of an explorer unwrapping a five-thousand-year-old mummy, she peeled back my foreskin. "Filth," she said, wrinkling her nose. "I am very much afraid you do not bathe properly, Trygve," she said.

She held my skinned-back penis between her thumb and forefinger as if it were a dead mouse. "Smegma," she said.

"Onk?" It occurred to me then, with the speed of sudden panic, that I had a dangerous medical problem no one had yet discovered.

"Smegma," she repeated. She took a cotton swab and lifted some of the white substance that had been protected under the foreskin.

Smegma, I thought. It seemed the perfect word for the white corruption that grew silently under the foreskin. If there existed an uglier word in the English language, I didn't know what it was.

"Don't you realize, Trygve," she said, as she finished swabbing away smegma, "that you could become in*fected?*"

I shook my head.

"An infection here could be extremely serious, Trygve. If it became bad enough, you could lose this little fellow."

She held the little fellow up, contemplating its danger-ridden future. "From smegma to gangrene. Then it's too late. Off it must come, like any other diseased organ."

"Onk?"

"Yes. *Off,*" she said.

All the heat her gentle ministrations had generated left me. I felt cold even under the warmth of the freshly wrung-out wash-cloth as she finished giving me my bath.

Back in the hospital in the outskirts of London, her husband or boyfriend discovered his legs were gone. He shouted in the night with a weak and cracking voice for a nurse. "My *legs,*" he sobbed. "What have they done with my *legs?*"

"Hush hush," the night nurse lullabied. "You'll wake the others."

"But my *legs…*"

"Gangrene, Lieutenant," she said, sitting on the edge of his bed and picking up his cold, trembling hand. "Your legs had to be sacrificed. The doctors had no choice, no choice at all."

The nurse finished with me and tucked me in. She was singing again, the same sad-sounding song that shouldn't have been sad-sounding since it was about the war finally ending and all the soldiers coming home for good.

↓

The girl in the bed next to mine was weak but cheerful. "My name's Hildy," she said, smiling at me. She was too weak to lift her head from the pillow and smiling was such an effort that her eyes closed and she fell asleep after telling me her name. She woke up in a few minutes and said, "I've got leukemia."

"Onk?" I said.

"Leukemia," she repeated. "It has something to do with my blood. It doesn't work right."

Her eyes closed again. She had a big Raggedy Ann doll. She slept with her arm around the doll. Later that day her parents came to visit her. There was a priest with them. The priest sat in a chair next to Hildy's bed and whispered something to her. He bowed his head then and rubbed his forehead with his fingertips. He reminded me of a priest I saw in a Bela Lugosi movie. The priest in the movie held up a large wooden crucifix to stop Bela Lugosi from taking the girl he'd had his eyes on, but Bela Lugosi only laughed at the priest and his wooden crucifix. Hildy's mother touched the corners of her eyes with a hanky. Her husband, a heavyset man in a green suit, stood nervously at the foot of the bed, shifting his weight from one foot to the other.

"Don't cry, Mommy," Hildy said. "I've got Raggedy."

Hildy's father turned his back to his wife and daughter. He raised his head and closed his eyes tight. He looked mad. His big hands opened and closed. A small convulsion lifted his shoulders.

Hildy fell asleep. After another minute or so, her parents and the priest left. Before she left, Hildy's mother pulled the blanket up around Hildy's neck then kissed her forehead and cheeks.

I fell asleep too and dreamed of Dracula. Blood was on his mind, my blood and Hildy's blood. He was in the ward, his big black cape flying behind him as if the hospital were filled with wind. I tried to yell for help but the string at the back of my mouth hurt so badly I couldn't manage a loud enough yell to attract anyone's notice.

When I woke up, Hildy was looking at me with her dark, lusterless eyes. She was about my age, maybe a year older, but the look in her eyes made her seem adult. Her eyes were calm and indifferent, like those of an adult who had adult things to think about.

"What grade are you in?" Hildy asked me.

I held up my right hand and showed her five fingers.

"Fifth," she said. "Five-A."

I nodded.

"I'll be in six-A," she said.

She was pretty, even though her arms and neck were splotched and her eyes had no shine to them. I decided to show her how to encode messages. I pushed myself up to a sitting position, and swung my legs out of the bed. It made me dizzy and I had to steady myself for a few seconds. The chilly tiles of the floor were a shock, and I realized that I hadn't been on my feet for over a day. My knees buckled when I stood and I had to catch myself on the edge of the bed. But when I looked over at Hildy again, she was asleep.

"Hey, kid," said the boy in the body cast.

"Onk," I said.

"Since you're up and around, how about coming over here. My foot itches like hell, and I can't scratch it."

I walked around the foot of my bed. His feet were sticking out of two plaster tubes. He had to lie flat on his back, immobilized. The plaster covered his pelvis and torso and neck. His arms up to the wrists were plastered, the right one suspended in midair about a foot above the bed. There was a hole at his crotch, big enough for a hand to fit in. I imagined the singing nurse running her thrilling washcloth around inside of that dark cave, searching for smegma. I wondered how he stood it.

"The right foot," he said. "Along the side, just above the heel. Don't use your fingernails, that'll drive me nuts. Use that piece of sandpaper tied to the foot of the bed."

A piece of gritty sandpaper dangled from the foot of his bed by a piece of string. I sandpapered his foot where he'd asked me to. The foot twitched and jumped.

"Jesus," he said, "do it harder. Otherwise it tickles."

I sanded hard enough to draw blood, and that seemed to satisfy him.

"Thanks," he said. "I'm glad you're here. You're going to come in handy, kid."

That evening, Mitchell, Mother, and Aunt Ginger came to see me. William had taken Betty to a baseball game again.

"How's the hemophiliac?" Mitchell asked.

I looked at him, then at Mother.

"He's not a hemophiliac," Mother said. "For God's sake, don't get his imagination going. You know how he is."

This was news to me. Mother thought I had an imagination. I was both flattered and disturbed to find out that I was the subject of Mother's *opinion*. Flattered to be thought about; disturbed because being thought about created distance. She *thought* about me the way an astronomer might think about the rings of Saturn.

Aunt Ginger put her hand on my wrinkled brow and smoothed it. "He's got a fine imagination," she said. But Aunt Ginger also spoke of me as if I weren't there, even though her cool hand stroked my forehead.

"Imagination can be dangerous," Mitchell said. "The nuthouse is full of people with too much imagination."

"That's right," Mother said. "So why do you bring up hemophilia? Now he'll think about bleeding to death whenever he gets a cut or scrape, that's how his imagination works."

"Okay," Mitchell said, "he doesn't have hemophilia. He's just a bleeder."

Suddenly they were all looking at me, as if they realized I was *there*, in the hospital bed, listening to them.

"Ahnzome," I said.

"What?" Mitchell said, bending close to me.

"He said he wants to go home," Aunt Ginger said.

"You can't go home yet," Mother said. "They want to make sure the infection is gone. Otherwise we'd just have to bring you back when you started bleeding again."

"It really could be hemophilia," Mitchell said to Mother, as if I were as far away as the rings of Saturn.

Mother looked exasperated. "If it was hemophilia, don't you think they would have told us by now?"

"They would if they'd *tested* him for it," Mitchell said. "Who's to say they tested for it?"

"You don't have hemophilia," Aunt Ginger said, leaning down to me. She kissed my forehead.

"Ahnzome," I said.

"You *can't* and that's that," Mitchell said.

I closed my eyes and howled. It was a brain-howl, not involving my swollen soft palate. I howled in my brain like Lon Chaney howled at the full moon when he realized the truth of his situation. It was a lonely howl, a howl that should have made the audience sad, not frightened. It should have made them weep, not tremble.

↓

"Your blood is mine," Bela Lugosi said.

"No it isn't," I said.

He sat on my bed. "Be reasonable, Monk," he said.

"My blood is *my* blood," I insisted.

He smiled indulgently. "If you could only hear how ridiculous you sound," Bela Lugosi said.

He was confusing me. "A vampire will say anything to get what he wants," I said.

"You're not being germane," he said.

When he bent down to get at my throat, I woke up.

I sat up in bed and looked around the darkened ward. The dream was so vivid and undreamlike that I felt Count Dracula could be anywhere in the ward, hiding.

"Hildy?" I whispered, ignoring the string cutting my palate.

"What," she said.

I was glad to see that she was awake. "Someone *there?*" I said. Tears filled my eyes from the pain of articulation.

"No, no one," she said. "Just me and Raggedy."

Then she began snoring. She sounded like an old person. Her breathing seemed crusty with age.

Though I wouldn't let myself fall back asleep, I couldn't stop thinking about my dream of Dracula. What did he mean, "Your blood is mine"? Why did he think I was being ridiculous denying it?

My blood *is* my blood, I said to myself. It's in me, flowing through me, keeping me alive. I own it. It's mine. No one else can have it.

This made me think of transfusions. There was such a thing as "blood types." I was an O positive. There were O negatives and A positives and negatives and for all I knew there was an entire alphabet soup of blood types. The thing was, there had to be a limited number of types and large numbers of human beings shared each type. My O-positive blood would work in the veins of someone else with O-positive blood. In that case, my blood was his blood. If there were a hundred million people in the world with O-positive blood, then my blood was their blood and their blood was mine.

Blood ownership became a real problem for me that night. I wanted to shut off my mind but I couldn't. Blood was only a small part of the problem. You could look at bone the same way, and flesh. You could look at hearts, lungs, livers, kidneys, and intestines exactly the same way. If it were possible to look at all your internal parts lined up next to someone else's internal parts, could you tell the difference? Could you say, That's *me* and that over there is *him?* You couldn't.

So Dracula was right. If there were monsters that fed on bone, they could make the same argument: I'm sorry, but this bone is mine. A liver monster could say, This liver belongs to me. The brain could be snapped out of its skull-shell like a clam by brain monsters, and so on.

But if Dracula took my blood, he also took my life. That much was true, at least.

But what was my life?

My life was something that blood, flesh, bone, and all the internal organs made possible. Without the parts of my body, where would "I" be?

I thought hard about my body. I liked it. But was any of it mine? Was I my liver? Was I my heart and lungs? Was I my skeleton or the meat that covered my skeleton? Was I the skin that covered my meat? Was I the intelligible noise blown past my vocal cords by my lungs?

Yes. No.

Were the three long hairs that grew out of the back of my hand *me?*

No. None of it was me. Yes. All of it was me.

This thing I called "me," was it the sum of all my parts?

My heart didn't like the direction of my thoughts and began to beat hard and fast. I broke into a sweat and had to kick off the blankets. *Think of something else,* I told myself. I put myself into the cockpit of a Dauntless Dive Bomber. On the horizon I saw the black smoke of a Jap cruiser. I climbed to attack altitude and began my bomb run. Tracers streamed up at me from the cruiser. I tried to attach my fear to the fear of combat, but it wasn't working. I was afraid of myself, not of the imaginary Japs.

In spite of my effort to stay awake, I fell asleep again. Hildy got out of her bed and sat on the edge of mine. "I have to have your blood," she said.

"My blood is mine," I said, and I knew it was a lie.

"Help me," she said.

She bent down to me and put her mouth on my neck. I felt her small teeth sink in.

I gave up arguing against it. As she sucked my blood, I fell like a stone into deeper sleep. It was a black dream of nothing. Miles and eons of nothing enveloped me. My hammering heart catapulted me out of this dream like a Douglas Dauntless being catapulted off the deck of an attack carrier.

But I didn't wake up. I was back in the first dream, with Hildy. She was lying in her bed and a priest was murmuring something to her. He had a crucifix with him, a big wooden crucifix like the one the priest in the Dracula movie had used to ward off evil. Except that it was different. It was part crucifix, part Kilroy drawing. The priest held it up so that all the children in the ward could see it. It looked like this:

The priest growled. I knew him. He was Sylvester Snell in priest's garb. I prayed at the top of my lungs because I knew that each of us in the children's ward was in extreme peril. My throat hurt like crazy as the string rasped against my soft palate, but I didn't hold back. I had to scream my prayer because a brief vision of The Supreme Being up in heaven had flashed across my mind: He was an ancient old man asleep on his arm, and the beautiful angels didn't seem to be worried. They went on playing their soothing lullabies on their silver harps while our old Supreme Being snored.

When I woke up it was late morning. Hildy was gone and her bed had been stripped. The thin mattress had been folded in half. The naked bed springs gleamed in morning light.

The meaning of this entered my mind gradually, and then with stunning force.

I remembered my dream then. It came to me in clear images, and I saw that it made perfect sense. The Supreme Being was old, too old to keep himself interested in us. Watching over us all through history had made him sleepy and bored. What else could account for the state of the world?

Maybe in the days of Adam and Eve he'd been wide awake. In those days everything was new and interesting and he kept tabs on each of us and nothing happened without a good reason.

There was no good reason for Hildy's death.

Not one.

↓

Mother brought me home the following afternoon, after her shift at Douglas. I'd only been in the hospital for three days but it seemed longer. Something had changed at home. I didn't know what it was but it made me feel that I'd been away for months. I went into my bedroom. It was a mess, but then it always had been a mess. I checked my shortwave radio for tampering. It was fine. I picked up KTK immediately, the naval radio station up in San Francisco. KTK played a prerecorded message in Morse code over and over. CQ CQ CQ DE KTK KTK KTK AR. Then it gave the frequencies it operated on, plus a series of numbers and letters that I assumed were encoded messages meant for the ears of the Pacific fleet alone. Malcolm and I had tried to break this code many times but always came up with nonsense phrases. We once converted a series of numbers and letters to: High Fools Leap In Time. It was the closest we ever came to a sensible message.

I listened to the regular rhythms of KTK, trying to figure out what was different in our household. I glanced around the messy bedroom, expecting to see the obvious change—maybe the walls had been painted, or the quilt on the bed had been replaced, or the curtains, and so on—but I only saw the same walls, the same unmade bed, comic books lying open on the floor, the same curtains blowing in the window, William's B B gun leaning in a corner, the same overhead light fixture with its collection of dead bugs, and the same stale cigarette-smoke air. Nothing at all unusual.

I shut off the radio and took off my earphones. I went to the dresser mirror and took a careful look at myself. Maybe I was the one who had changed. I had no color. My eyes looked like they had sunk deeper into their sockets. My lips looked thin and bloodless.

I had a vampire look. My mind was blank, but my expression was that of someone who had been following a long and intricate line of thought. I hooked my fingers into the corners of my mouth and pulled my lips into a grotesque grin that exposed my Transylvanian teeth to the molars.

I wasn't supposed to play for a few more days but I felt good enough to be bored with myself. I walked up to the Bruckners' apartment and knocked. The door wasn't latched and it opened slightly. I pushed it open a little more and peeked inside.

The apartment was empty. All the furniture was gone. There were some boxes and scraps of old newspapers lying scattered around. There was a mop and bucket in the hall. The bucket still had gray water in it. There was a dirty sock in the kitchen. I found one of Betty's algebra tests from the previous school year behind a radiator.

I went into the living room where Malcolm and I had listened to so many radio programs. I remembered Betty's breasts glistening in this room and her sharp tongue scolding us. Her piano was gone. The big Zenith was gone.

"Hey!" I yelled. "Hey, Malc!" My voice echoed on the bare walls. My palate still hurt and so I didn't yell again.

I found William on the roof of the apartment building. The roof was flat, the edges guarded by a wall three feet high. William was sitting on the guard wall, his feet dangling over the side. He spit with artistic precision toward the street three stories down and twenty feet out.

"Where did the Bruckners go?" I said.

William shrugged.

He had his roll of zinc pennies. He opened and closed his fist on the roll of pennies and I realized that he was in one of his dangerous moods.

"Looks like they moved," I said. I tried my luck at spitting, but the gob of saliva flew apart in the air and sprayed back into my face.

"No shit," William said.

"I don't get it," I said.

William arced a stream of spit into the top of a date palm. "Hobarth found out they were Jews," he said.

"Hobarth? The guy in the big car? He made them move out?"

"He made Sturdevant make them move out."

Sturdevant, the manager, was a mousy man who always wore carpet slippers. He always seemed to be listening to noises in his own head. He would walk through the halls of the apartment building with his head cocked and his lips pursed.

"Sturdevant couldn't make a fly move out," I said.

"He begged them," William said. "His wife baked a cake. Sturdevant brought up the cake and then begged them to leave. If they didn't go, then the Sturdevants would be kicked out. That's what he said, anyway. The fucker bawled."

"It's not fair," I said.

William laughed but didn't say anything. I looked around the big empty roof. Malcolm and I had planned to build a giant rectangle-shaped antenna, strung from corner to corner, so that we could pick up stations in India and China. We were going to have two separate lead-in wires, one for the Bruckners' Zenith, one for my two-tube kit radio. "Monk, we'll drag in stations on Mars with an antenna like that," Malcolm had said.

"So they just *left?*" I said, unable to believe that someone like Sturdevant or even Hobarth could make people like the Bruckners do what they wanted them to do.

"They had to. It's the law. No Jews means no Jews, period."

"Even so," I said.

"Mr. Bruckner wanted to leave anyway. He wanted to go back to Grumman, on Long Island. He said that's where they belonged. He didn't think much of L.A."

"He worked for Grumman?"

"He's an engineer. He helped design the Wildcat. He said he wanted to go back and work on the new version of the Wildcat, called the Hellcat."

I'd seen pictures of the new carrier-based fighter plane, the Grumman Hellcat. It was sleek and beautiful and had eight .50-caliber machine guns. It flew higher and faster than the Zero, almost as high and as fast as the P-38 Lightning. The Lightning's big disadvantage was that it had to be based on land, and so its combat area was limited. The Hellcat could fight anywhere. It occurred to me that if Mr. Bruckner had stayed at Lockheed, he could have helped design a carrier-based Lightning. Now *that* would have been something to see. But Hobarth had made that impossible.

"Is Hobarth working for the Japs?" I said.

"What?" William spit, then looked at me in the way he always did, like I was a nut.

"He could be a spy," I said.

"The Monk is coming unglued," William said. "The Monk is on his way to Napa."

"No, really," I said. "If you think about it. I mean, what if Lockheed was trying to make a carrier-based P-38 and Mr. Bruckner knew all about how to do it and stuff?"

"Monk," William said.

"What?"

"Shut up."

He slid off the guard wall and left the roof. I saw a scrap of paper where he'd been sitting. It was a note, written on violet-colored paper. It said, "I love you and always will." It was signed "B.B." Betty Bruckner.

⊻

It didn't matter to Mitchell that Garland Quince and Jack Twilly were frauds who had taken him for one hundred dollars, a book of gas stamps, and some choice cuts of black market beef before they were through with him. It didn't matter that Franchot Tone would never come to our apartment, or that he was not going to hear anything about the leading-man potential of Mitchell Self-age. When the telegram came from the president of the United States, nothing at all mattered to Mitchell beyond his immediate bleak future. He lost interest in everything. He was depressed, frightened, and couldn't even make himself go to work. After his pre-induction physical—which he had insisted was only a formality everyone between the ages of eighteen and thirty-five had to go through—he'd been drafted into the army.

"Greetings from the President of the United States," the telegram began. It went on to say that Mitchell had been selected to serve his country. It explained, briefly, his patriotic duty, and then told him where to report and on what day. On July 1st, he was to report to the army's induction center in downtown Los Angeles where he'd be transported, by bus, to Fort Ord.

"At least Fort Ord is in California," Mother said. "We'll be able to visit." She wasn't at all shocked by the telegram.

Mitchell regarded her with resentment. "Basic training only lasts eight weeks," he said.

"It's close to San Francisco, isn't it?" Mother said. "We could visit you weekends and see the sights. I've never been to Chinatown."

"I like the Bay Area," Aunt Ginger said.

"Oh for Christ's sakes!" Mitchell said, jumping up from the dinner table. "I'm probably going to be killed and all you two can talk about is sightseeing!"

Mother sighed. "I just meant if you're going to be at Ford Ord why shouldn't we all have some fun before you . . . leave?"

We were having sherbet for dessert. William had finished his and was reading the funnies. He looked up at me now and then and made a comical face. He didn't have much respect for Mitchell and now whatever respect he did have was completely erased by Mitchell's squirming terror at the idea of having to go into combat.

"Something strike you as being funny, Trygve?" Mitchell said.

I didn't realize that I'd been smiling at William's comical faces.

"No," I said. "I don't think so."

Mitchell looked at all of us then like we were part of the conspiracy that was sending him off to war. "I'm going out," he said.

"Tell your girlfriend hello," Mother said in an offhand way.

Mitchell looked at her for a long frozen moment, then he looked at me. It occurred to me that Mother was referring to Millie, the "cousin" who lived by MacArthur Park, and that the look I was getting from Mitchell accused me of blabbing his secret. But I hadn't.

Mitchell slammed the door as he left. We went back to our sherbet. The only sound in the apartment was the clink of our spoons against the glass bowls.

"Her name is Millie," I said.

Mother looked at me. It was a cold, fatalistic look, charged with a small pique of curiosity.

"She's nice," I said.

"Too bad for her, then," Mother said.

William and I cleared the table, then went into our room. I plugged in a coil for the forty-nine-meter band and searched the dial for ships at sea. I picked up someone screaming Spanish. He would scream for a few seconds, pause, then scream again. I pictured a humble fishing boat. The captain of the fishing boat had spotted a Jap sub off the coast of California and was trying to report it. But he couldn't speak English. He was Mexican and couldn't make himself understood to the United States Navy. "Run for it," I said. "Run for it."

"The Monk is talking to the radio again," William said.

He smiled at me, though, and I knew he wasn't annoyed. He still had a goofy, comical expression on his face. Since he'd turned sixteen, he'd started a mustache. It looked like a dirt smudge. The bristles were widely spaced, the hair black and coarse.

"Want to see something, Monk?" he said.

"Sure," I said, slipping off the headphones.

He rolled up his sleeve to the shoulder. High up on his thin arm there was a tattoo. It was a heart with "B.B." inside.

"Where did you get it?" I asked.

"Tijuana. Betty and I went there while you were in the hospital. We were supposed to be at Ocean Park pier, but we took the bus to San Ysidro and walked over the border."

He amazed me. I wondered what other amazing things he'd do in his lifetime.

"I got something else, too," he said. He went to the closet and took out a shoe box. The box was full of his personal things—a picture of his real mother, some old letters, Canadian coins, a tie clip with a diamond in it that had belonged to his grandfather. Lying in the middle of all this was a carefully folded paper. He unfolded it and showed it to me.

Bureau of Records and Statistics
Department of Health

CERTIFICATION OF BIRTH

This is to certify that WILLIAM HAROLD FERGUS, sex MALE, was born in the city of FREZNO, CALIFORNIA, on JUNE 10, 1925, according to Birth Record No. 17632 filed in the Frezno office of the Bureau on JUNE 15, 1925. In witness thereof, the seal of the Department of Health of the City of Frezno, California has been affixed hereto this 18 day of JUNE, 1925.

K-999943 _____Director of Bureau

"What is it?" I said.

"What does it look like?"

I stared at it for a while, trying to make sense of it.

"Dammit, Monk, it's a birth certificate. I had it done in Teejay. It cost me five bucks is all."

It looked authentic:

It had been printed on thick, expensive-looking paper, with a marbled surface. Staring at it, I realized exactly what it meant. He was going to make good on his promise to join the marines, even though he was only sixteen, a full two years short of the age certified by this phony piece of paper.

"They spelled Fresno wrong," I said.

He snatched the paper out of my hand. "What do you mean?" he said, his eyes scanning each fraudulent word hotly.

"There's no zee in it," I said. "It's spelled with an ess."

"Bullshit," he said.

"No, really. The ess sounds like a zee, but it's an ess all the same."

William folded the certificate carefully and put it back in the shoe box. He carried the shoe box back to the closet.

"It doesn't matter," he said. "It'll work. No one's going to get excited over a goddamned zee."

"Maybe," I said.

"Maybe *shit*. And if they do, I'll go back to Teejay and get another one. It's not that hard, Monk. Nothing's that hard. All you've got to do is want it bad enough."

I went back to my radio. The screaming man was gone. In his place a marimba band was playing the carioca. The music faded in and out. It seemed to lap against my ears, like waves.

"It won't be long now, Monk," I heard William say.

But I didn't respond. I was alone, in the ocean, supported only by my life jacket. All my friends were gone and my ship was sunk.

↓

The movie *Lost Horizon* came to the Variety. Aunt Ginger wanted to see it and she asked me to go with her. I didn't especially want to go since I believed it was a serious adult movie with a lot of drawing room dialogue and I couldn't stand that. But Aunt Ginger convinced me otherwise. "There's an airplane crash in it," she said, "and the survivors wind up in a place where no one ever gets old." She made a plane of her small white hand and sailed it into the back cushion of the sofa we were sitting on. Her hand crumpled and fell to the seat. "Boom," she said. Her face was lit by a childlike enthusiasm I could not help responding to.

"Okay," I said. "It sounds good."

Ronald Colman wasn't the kind of actor I liked to see, but the story didn't sound boring, to hear Aunt Ginger tell it. I decided I could tolerate not seeing a Bela Lugosi or a Boris Karloff movie for once. The only other movies I liked were comedies by Abbott and Costello or Jack Oakie. Horror and slapstick comedy—I couldn't get enough of them—and of course war movies. Anything in between was too much like everyday life, and what was the point of that since everyday life was the boring thing you were faced with day to day?

Lost Horizon, though, turned out to be a kind of horror movie after all. I warmed up to it gradually and wound up loving it. It didn't terrify me in the way a Dracula movie could, but it did make me sad and uneasy. Watching the true age of the beautiful young girl from Shangri-La catch up to her as she tried to leave the lush valley shocked me. It was John Howard's fault, Ronald Colman's young, hotheaded brother. He loved the girl and she loved him and neither of them believed that she would die in a horrible manner if she tried to leave. Love made them foolish and irresponsible. They disregarded the truth. Ronald Colman knew better, but he couldn't make either of them listen to reason.

Once they were out of the safe valley and into the high mountains where a constant blizzard howled, the years began to tick off like seconds. The girl knew it would happen to her, but she was blinded by love and reckless hope. The crow's feet of middle age came; she couldn't keep pace with the porters; she begged to lie down in the snow and rest; dark hollows appeared under her eyes. At first you weren't sure it was actually happening. You didn't want to believe it. You wanted to believe that if they hurried, if they got over the pass and into the real world, then she'd be exempt from what had to be a local magic of limited reach.

But then her spine started to bend with the weight of the swiftly accumulating years. A delicate mist fogged her once vivacious eyes. Her hands trembled. "Go *back!*" I hissed. A woman seated in front of us turned around and said, "Hush! Be still!"

It was too late to go back. A fatal line had been crossed and the machinery of decay could not be shut off. The girl sank into the snow as John Howard and Ronald Colman stood helplessly by. "My darling," John Howard whispered, kneeling beside her, taking her scaly hand in his. She was old enough now to be his grandmother. All the suspended years fell on her with a vengeance.

The audience began to squirm. They coughed nervously. They shared a general feeling of saccharine despair. How could this movie have a happy ending? Audiences then demanded happy endings. The world was full of sad endings—movies, at least, should try to raise our hopes.

"Oh bull*shit!*" a man in back of me shouted as Lord Gainsford told the members of his London club how Bob Conway—Ronald Colman—fought his way back to Shangri-La, crossing impassable mountains by himself to be reunited with the girl he loved and the land he was destined to preside over as the new High Lama.

I didn't pay attention to this part of the movie. The movie, for me, ended in the mountain pass where the girl had swiftly aged. I replayed this part in my mind, increasing its poignancy. I watched the vengeful centuries exact their withering toll. Her once firm and voluptuous flesh sagged against her bones until it looked like tissue paper draped over sticks. Then the rags of her flesh lost whatever fibrous integrity they still had and began to tatter into pale ribbons. Her slender bones poked through: the arch of ribs, the grinning skull, the rugged spine. Seconds and centuries later, the bones grew porous. They gradually drifted down into little anthills of dust which were playfully scattered by the sub-zero wind. "By Jove, by Jove," the always cool Ronald

Colman said as his brother went mad and dashed away, stumbling into a yawning crevasse, where he died.

Aunt Ginger, I realized, was gripping my hand tightly. She squeezed hard enough to move the bones. It hurt. I looked at her. There were tears in her eyes. "It's a metaphor, Trygve," she said. "It's *our* metaphor."

I didn't know the word.

"It means you can't keep anything. It means you can't hold on. It means you might as well try to grab an armful of fog."

"Be quiet," the woman in front of us said.

"The movie, you mean," I said, catching on.

"Yes. The movie. *It's* the metaphor."

I had thought about the Dracula movies in exactly the same way. I squeezed Aunt Ginger's hand back to indicate my understanding. We were kindred spirits. I wanted to say this to her but didn't know how.

She quivered. Her hand jerked in mine. Her teeth chattered. "I've got to get out of here," she said, standing up. "Let's go. The rest of the movie can only be crap, anyway."

Out on the sidewalk, under the blazing marquee, she trembled convulsively. It was still warm out, in the high seventies, but she acted as though it were near freezing. She acted as though we were standing in a blizzard on a high mountain pass between Tibet and the actual world. She still held my hand in a death grip. Then she started walking, swiftly, jerkily, in the wrong direction.

"Where are we going?" I asked. I had to trot every so often to keep up with her.

"Nowhere. Absolutely nowhere. No one's going anywhere," she said.

"This isn't the way," I said.

She didn't answer. We walked for blocks at this terrific pace, as if some catastrophe would catch up with us if we dallied. We walked past neon-lit bars, diners, closed shops, and used-car lots. A man stepped out of a diner as we walked by. He rubbed his hands together at the sight of Aunt Ginger's pumping stride.

"Hubba-hubba," he growled.

"Simian," Aunt Ginger said.

I was out of breath. She dragged my weight along. "Stop," I said. "Wait a minute."

She looked at me. Her face expanded in the blazing hues of neon. Her eyes shot through me. "I knew you before," she said. "Do you believe me?" She was gazing across the centuries.

I shrugged. "We'd better go home," I said. "It's late."

"We were friends *then*, too."

"I know," I said. But I was being sly. I was humoring her. She knew it, though, and gave my arm a yank, as if to shock me awake.

"Stay clear of it," she said. "I'm telling you this. I have always been your friend."

"I know," I said, less slyly but still humoring her. I realized then that Mitchell was probably right about her.

"You *don't* know. You may never know. I just want you to remember what I'm telling you."

"Let's go home, Aunt Ginger," I said. It was a whining plea. "I'll make us some hot chocolate."

She laughed and let go of my hand. She touched my face. "Trygve," she said, "you don't have to worry about me. You just have to worry about yourself. Just remember to stay clear of it."

"Of *what?*" I said, annoyed. "Stay clear of *what?*"

She turned in a graceful circle, her upturned palm gesturing to the beautiful city of the angels.

She walked away from me. I watched her enter a bar. I followed her, but in the entryway of the bar a big man stopped me. He was breathing heavily through his mouth. When he saw me he winked. He dug into his coat pocket and took out a dime. He gave it to me. "Go get me a paper, kid," he said. "Be a good Scout. You don't mind, do you?"

"No sir," I said. "I don't mind."

I put the dime in my pocket and went home.

↓

I got a postcard from Malcolm. He'd sent it from Des Moines, Iowa: "Monk, The train stopped here for an hour, so I got this dumb card." (The card was a photograph of milk cows staring stupidly at a grinning boy in a straw hat.) "If you build our antenna, you should use number 12 wire, not 14 or 16. A long piece of 14 or 16 will probably break if it gets windy. Make sure you use insulated screw-eyes, excuse my French. Ha ha. Don't let the Japs bomb L.A." Then he added, in code, "$R^4A^1M^3A^1M^3D^1A^1R^4$ $P^4A^1E^1R^4N^3$ $H^2E^1R^4D^1$ K^3R^4."

I worked on the code for half an hour but didn't crack it. I turned on my radio and found nothing but static from one end of the dial to the other on all my shortwave bands. Hot summer days were bad for shortwave listening and I vowed to build the big antenna Malcolm and I had planned so that when the cool weather of fall came I'd be ready for India and China.

William came in and picked up my postcard. He glanced at it front and back, then tossed it back on the desk.

I knew what was troubling him: nothing from Betty. He flopped on the bed and picked up a comic book. I switched off the radio and went out.

I went up to the roof and paced off its length and width. It was ninety paces long and forty-six paces wide. I'd tried to make my paces one foot in length. To be on the safe side I added ten feet to each measurement. I added it all up and rounded the final figure off to three-twenty. Three hundred and twenty feet of copper wire.

Then it hit me: *copper.* You couldn't *get* copper. All available copper was needed for the war effort. That's why the government had minted zinc pennies!

"Oh *shit!*" I yelled.

I yelled it from the roof for the ears of the world. I yelled with my eyes shut and with no regard for my damaged throat. The girl from across the street looked up at me with the neutral eyes of practiced boredom. She was sitting on the lawn in white shorts and halter, sunning herself. Though she was only thirteen or fourteen, she had all the disdain for childhood enthusiasms a grown woman of the world would have.

I didn't care. I was too crushed to be shamed from the roof. I sat on the guard wall, my legs dangling over the side. It was a good thirty feet straight down. I didn't care. I sat loosely on the edge and stared at the rooftops of West L.A. I spit, but the violence of my effort caused it to spray. The girl looked up at me again and smiled faintly.

Out of a sense of desperation, I set out to find a hardware store. I walked eleven blocks down Wilshire Boulevard before I found one.

"I'd like three hundred and twenty feet of copper wire," I said, adding quickly, "It has to be twelve gauge."

The clerk smiled at me. "Wouldn't a lot of folks," he said.

I pulled wads of cash from my jeans. I'd been saving money from my allowance for weeks. I'd also gotten a five-dollar bill from my Italian grandmother in New York for my birthday, and I'd managed not to spend it.

"What other kind of wire do you have?" I said.

"Some fencing wire, some guy wire." He went to the back of the store and came back with a heavy coil of gray wire.

"What's it made of?" I said.

He shrugged. "It's wire. It's made of wire."

"I mean what *metal*. I want to use it for an antenna."

He drew a length of wire from the coil and bent it back and forth. "I guess it's steel, or iron. It should work, if all you want is a radio aerial. There's probably zinc and lead in it."

I bought two coils of the inferior wire and half a dozen insulated screw-eyes. Then I lugged it all home. I was still weak from my hospital stay and had to stop every so often to rest. The heavy gray wire turned my hands silver. I sat on a curb, looking at my silver hands. I tried to picture my antenna, strung from each corner of the apartment building like a big net. The net would catch the weakest of radio signals that fell out of the sky. I cupped my silver hands over my ears and imagined the new abundance of stations that would fill my earphones.

I had Malcolm's postcard with me. I took it out and tried deciphering his code again but got nowhere. I couldn't get past the numbers. I figured they had something to do with the order of the letters, but beyond that I didn't have a clue.

When I got home, Mitchell's Cadillac was parked out in front of the apartment building. William was behind the wheel. "Hop in," he said.

"Are you *nuts?*" I said. "Mitchell's home. He'll kill you."

"I'm driving him to the induction center. It's July first, remember? He's got to report."

"But you don't have a driver's license," I said. "You can't drive him."

He showed me a scrap of paper. It was a California driver's license, a black photostat complete with thumbprint. "Where'd you get *that?*" I said.

"Same place I got my birth certificate."

"Mitchell doesn't care?"

"Mitchell doesn't care about anything. He figures he's going off to be slaughtered anyway. He's kind of depressed."

The front door of the apartment building swung open and Mitchell came through it carrying a suitcase. Mother followed him out.

When she saw me, Mother said, "I told you to stick around the apartment today, Trygve. You knew Mitchell was leaving."

"I forgot," I said.

Mitchell opened the back door of the Cadillac and shoved his suitcase inside. Then he kissed Mother. It wasn't much of a kiss. I guess there was too much on his mind for enthusiastic kissing. Then he turned to me. "Goodbye, son," he said.

"Goodbye...Dad," I said.

My face got hot. I looked at my silver hands. We'd never been "son" or "Dad" to each other, and the enormity of the fiction we'd just agreed to rocked me with shame. It was a fiction with retroactive power. It made a movie out of the last six months. All that time he'd been "Dad." All that time I'd been "son."

Mitchell patted me on the head.

Mother sighed.

Mitchell and I shook hands in a manly way. "Look after things, Trygve," he said.

"I will," I said, my voice deepening automatically.

William started the Cadillac. Mitchell sat up front with William. They drove off. Mother and I raised our hands to wave but Mitchell didn't respond.

I carried my coils of wire into the apartment building. I tried to wash the silver coating off my hands but they only turned gray. They looked like the hands of a horror movie creature. I glanced at my face in the mirror above the sink and was surprised to see a smirk on it.

"Goodbye, 'son,'" the smirking face said.

"Goodbye, 'Dad,'" I replied.

"Look after things, Trygve," the smirker said.

"I will," I replied in my forced baritone voice.

I had discovered something about myself. I knew that I was now capable of mustering any necessary lie at will. I could say "Dad" and not mean it and I could accept being called "son" by someone who did not mean it. It was like discovering an unsuspected talent. William and Betty didn't have this talent, and I was dimly aware that it was a deficiency that would cost them dearly. I was also dimly aware that if this talent could be used without shame, its power would be awesome.

And dangerous. As dangerous to the one who used it as leukemia. Because necessary lies trick the liar himself. He *wants* to believe them. Then he does.

"Stay clear of it," Aunt Ginger had said.

Her words repeated themselves in my mind, gathering meaning.

↓

Uncle Gerald came home elated. He'd been at sea over a month and had not seen a single enemy submarine, airplane, or warship. It had been like a pleasure cruise. To celebrate, he took all of us out to see Ken Murray's Blackouts at the El Capitan theater in Hollywood. I didn't get most of the jokes and the skits bored me, but the adults were amused. Even William, who had other things on his mind, laughed out loud now and then. After the show we had Chinese food at Don the Beachcomber's. Uncle Gerald had several drinks before dinner but he didn't get nasty. His good mood held its own against the transforming power of alcohol. He kissed Aunt Ginger tenderly, with honest affection, and he kissed Mother in the same way. He told funny stories about exotic ports of call and he explained to William and me exactly how depth charges worked and how to take evasive action against a stalking sub.

His good mood continued the next day. Usually, in his sullen moods, he didn't notice much of what was going on around him. But now his eyes sparkled with a lively interest in all of us. When he saw me carrying my coils of wire through the apartment, he asked what I was up to. I told him about my plan to build the giant antenna Malcolm and I had designed. He immediately became curious. "Maybe I can be of some help," he said.

We went up to the roof. I dropped my heavy coils of gray wire and unfastened the ties that kept them from springing free and unraveling. I dug the insulated screw-eyes out of my pockets and lined them up next to the coils.

"Fine," Uncle Gerald said, "but I have one small question."

I looked at him. "What are you going to hang it on?" he said.

I hadn't given the details much thought. "Well, I thought I'd lay the wire on the guard wall, running it through the screw-eyes."

Uncle Gerald shook his dark head. "Half-assed, half-assed," he said. "If you're going to do this, then give it enough respect to do it right. If you just let the wire lay on the wall, then you'll pick up all sorts of interference, especially in bad weather."

I watched him pace the roof—inspecting the corners, glancing up at the sky from time to time—depressed by his criticism.

"Masts, Trygve," he said. "You'll want *masts*."

"Masts? You mean poles?"

"To hell with poles. Poles are for clotheslines. You want masts— *spars,* lad—big sturdy chaps to hang your wire from."

"But I don't have any masts. Where would I get masts?"

He stared into the distance. While he stared, he reached absently into his coat pocket and pulled out a silver flask. He unscrewed the cap, absently, and raised it to his lips. He took a few swallows, his eyes still reading the Pacific horizon. He lowered the flask. "You leave that to me, Tryg," he said.

He took the Cadillac out and was gone for hours. When he came back it was past suppertime. We'd eaten without him. He came into the apartment drunk, his hair wild, his eyes shining. Aunt Ginger wouldn't look at him. She was nervous around him even though he still seemed to be in a good humor.

"Come on, Tryg," he said. "We've got work ahead of us. Look, there's still two hours of daylight. Let's set to it, lad."

I looked at Mother. She had been paging through a copy of *Life* magazine. She glanced up briefly at me, then at Uncle Gerald, but said nothing.

"You should eat something," Aunt Ginger said.

"Oh, my darling," Uncle Gerald said. "I am well fed, my darling. I take nourishment from the sight of you, dear. The fragrance that surrounds you is my meat and bread, my sweetheart, my Ginger."

For some reason these words, though spoken without any sort of mockery or edginess, seemed to terrify Aunt Ginger. Her face grew pale and she shuddered visibly. She got up and smoothed her hands against her dress. Uncle Gerald went to her and took her in his big arms. She began to cry.

"Now, Ginger," he said. "Now, my darling. There's no need of these tears."

Mother sighed and got up. She went into the kitchen. I followed her. "What's wrong with Uncle Gerald?" I asked.

"He's drunk," she said.

"No, it's something else." I groped for the right words. "He's not *mad* at anybody."

"Look again, Trygve," Mother said in a bored tone of voice as she reheated the pot of coffee.

I went out. The Cadillac was parked at the front of the apartment building. It looked like a lumber truck. There were what looked like four skinned trees, an ax, and a bucksaw lashed on top of the big car. In the back seat a pile of hardware—rope, pulleys, boxes of nails, braided steel wire almost as thick as cable, and heavy porcelain insulators—filled the entire legroom area.

William came up behind me. "A lot of gear for a little two-tube radio," he said.

"I don't *want* all this," I said.

"You don't want all what?" Uncle Gerald said. I hadn't seen him come out of the apartment building. He stood between William and me. He slung his arms over our shoulders. My knees buckled.

"Isn't it going to be too big?" I asked, steadying myself.

"Nonsense," he said. "The bigger the better, when it comes to radio aerials. It's like a telescope, Tryg. The larger the lens of a telescope, the more light it gathers in. This is exactly the same principle. You want to be able to sweep the skies of every little radio wave. I'm going to build you a first-class aerial, much the same as the one on my ship. What do you say to that, lad?"

What *could* I say to that? The idea of a professional-looking antenna topping the apartment building thrilled me. It also scared me. A structure like that, supported by skinned trees high above the roof of the building, had to be illegal in some way. Or, if not actually illegal, then against the rules of the apartment building's owner, Mr. Hobarth. When he saw what I had done to his property, he'd have a fit. The notion of Mr. Hobarth gasping in rage at the sight of my antenna satisfied me in a way that nothing before ever had. It was Malcolm Bruckner's antenna, too. The satisfaction I felt was for Malcolm. I named the antenna Malcolm's Revenge, even before it was built.

Uncle Gerald changed into his dungarees and work shirt. He untied the ropes holding the skinned trees to the roof of the Cadillac then slid them off carefully. When he had one end of a tree down on the pavement, he'd find the balancing point and lift it in his arms. The trees about twenty feet long and were at least six inches in diameter at the base, tapering to about three inches at the top. Uncle Gerald carried each tree to the side of the apartment building and leaned it upright against the stucco wall. Then he unloaded the back seat of the Cadillac, and the three of us carried all the gear upstairs to the roof.

"How do we get the trees up here?" I asked.

"The masts you mean," Uncle Gerald said. He was sweating heavily and his face was red. "We'll haul them up the side of the building, lad." He picked up a coil of rope and carried it to the edge of the roof. He leaned on the guard wall and dropped the coil of rope over the side, keeping one end of it in his fist. "Now, William," he said. "I want you to go down there and secure the rope to the spar, near the top. Tryg and I will haul it up to the roof."

William left the roof and soon appeared below us. He set one of the skinned trees down and tied the rope to the tapered end. Then he stood up and stepped away from it. "Haul away," he said.

Uncle Gerald heaved mightily on the rope, gathering it in, hand over hand. The tree rose from the ground until it was vertical. I tried to get a handhold on the rope, but there was no room for me. Uncle Gerald crowded the guard wall with his bulk. The bones in his thick wrists stood out like white stones and the veins in his neck bulged dangerously purple as he dragged the tree up the side of the building. When the top of the tree appeared at the edge of the guard wall, Uncle Gerald clamped his big hand around it and grunted. His face darkened with strain, his eyes were shut tight. It looked like he was strangling some kind of long-necked creature with milk-white skin. "Help me," he groaned, but there was no room for me at the wall. He bent his knees, sucked air, and hoisted.

In this way, Uncle Gerald raised all the masts for my antenna to the rooftop of the apartment building.

His work shirt was black with sweat. He took his flask out of his pants pocket and uncapped it. He offered it to me. When I reached for it he held it away. "Not yet, Tryg," he said. "Not yet." Then he took a lengthy drink, his sweat-slick throat working. He sat down cross-legged and drank again.

"That's all we'll do today," he said. "Tomorrow the serious work begins. By the way, the wire you bought isn't any good, Tryg. We'll need copper. Good copper wire."

"You can't *get* copper," I said. "No one has any copper."

"It must be copper," he said. "We must use nothing less than copper. The stuff you have here doesn't have enough conductivity. It will resist the small amounts of electricity generated by the radio waves, Tryg. At such low levels of electricity, you can't afford unnecessary resistance."

"But I told you—"

"You told me your resourcefulness is wanting, lad."

He winked at me and a new fear tingled my neck hairs. I hadn't even thought to ask him *where* he got the trees, but that question, and now a new question, nagged at my mind: Where would he get *copper* wire? Whose trees had he chopped down?

He finished the remaining whisky in his flask and stood up. The evening sky had deepened to smoky blue. "I've got my land legs," he said.

To prove this was so, he climbed up on the guard wall and, like a high-wire performer, walked away from me, his arms outspread for balance.

↯

Aunt Ginger had put a Hildegarde record on the Victrola. Hildegarde sang, "Darling, *je vous aime beaucoup, je ne sais pas* what to do ... You have stolen my heart." The volume was up high and Aunt Ginger was sitting next to the machine holding her face in her hands.

Mother was in the kitchen, drinking coffee at the dining table. "What's wrong with Aunt Ginger?" I asked.

Mother sighed. "She's afraid."

"But Uncle Gerald is in a great mood. I've never seen him so happy," I said.

"Where *is* Gerald?" she asked, ignoring my argument.

"He's, uh, on the roof."

"What's he doing up there?"

"He's just *up* there. Walking around. He's got his land legs."

Aunt Ginger came in. Her face was streaked but she had stopped crying. "Did he say that?" she said. "Did he say he's got his land legs?"

"Yes," I said. "He said that. Then he started walking along the edge of the roof, on top of the guard wall."

Aunt Ginger's face went white. "Oh no," she said. She ran out of the apartment. Mother followed her. William came out of our bedroom.

"What's going on?" he said.

"Search me," I said.

William and I went outside. Mother and Aunt Ginger were standing out in the street looking up at the roof of the apartment building. "Come down, come *down*," Aunt Ginger pleaded.

Uncle Gerald was still walking along the guard wall, but now his hands were in his pockets. He was whistling a lively jump tune and every now and then he'd do a little dance step.

"I've got my land legs!" he shouted. He was a thick black figure against the darkening sky.

"Please come down!" Aunt Ginger said.

"You'll fall," Mother added.

Uncle Gerald laughed. He recited a little poem:

> I'm the one salt tar
> That will walk a spar
> Drunk as a pagan god
> Under the northern star.

"Don't!" Aunt Ginger yelled. *"Don't!"*

"I won't!" Uncle Gerald laughed back. "I *won't!*"

Then he stepped down off the wall. "What's troubling you?" he said, leaning on the wall with his elbows.

"You're scaring the hell out of her," Mother said.

The black figure leaning on the wall said, "I think not. I think the source of fear is other than yours truly."

William and I went back inside. I picked up the *Life* magazine

Mother had been reading and thumbed through it. It was a special issue devoted to combat photographs in full color of the war in the south Pacific. There was a full-page picture of a marine whose left side had been torn away by the blast of a cannon shell. The entire left half of his body was a ragged red pulp. The other half was normal-looking. The normal-looking half, in the instant of the photograph, still believed it was alive. The normal-looking half held a rifle high, the running leg dug for traction in the sandy beach. The half-face that was normal-looking showed a fierce eye, and the half-mouth showed teeth that were set for battle.

Aunt Ginger came in. She sat next to me. "I dreamed of him," she said, indicating the blown-up marine. "Last night, before I saw this magazine, I dreamed of a half-man. He was wandering around in the street. I called to him from the window but he only glanced at me. He acted as though I were an ordinary thing, like a bird in a tree. I tried to warn him of some real danger, but he only shook his head, as if to clear his one ear of water."

Mother came in then and put a Jimmy Dorsey record on the Victrola. "I'm going to get cheerful," she said. "If anyone wants to join me, that's their business." She made herself a rum and Coke and slid the *Life* magazine under the couch.

A half hour later Uncle Gerald came in. He was dripping wet. He shook his head, clearing it of water. His feet were bare.

Aunt Ginger gripped my arm hard enough to cut off the circulation.

"I took a little walk in the rain," he said. "There I was, staring up at the stars in the rain." He laughed and ran his handkerchief over his neck and face. "No clouds, no rain. It was a mistake. I was standing in the spray of a lawn sprinkler, thinking of Vancouver and how nice it would be this time of year."

A smile full of reverie split his red face. His feet, I noticed, were white as paper, as if they'd been under water for a month. Aunt Ginger's grip on my arm relaxed. She slumped into the sofa.

↓

Uncle Gerald pulled down the Murphy bed and put Aunt Ginger on it. He knelt beside the bed and rubbed her hand. She came around after a minute to an unfamiliar world. She looked at the faces surrounding her with no recognition in her eyes. She looked at her own hands. Puzzlement furrowed her brow. She sat up, looked at Uncle Gerald again, and then it all came back to her. Uncle Gerald took her in his arms and said, "There, now, little Ingrid," and smoothed her silky blond hair with his big hand.

"Ingrid?" I whispered to Mother.

"Yes," she said. " 'Ginger' is a nickname for 'Ingrid.' "

This amazed me. Someone had given her the nickname "Ginger" just as I had been given the nickname "Monk." But hers had been given thoughtlessly. I liked "Monk" and felt that it fit me in some way. But "Ginger" seemed too frivolous for a serious, book-reading person like my aunt. They should have let her keep Ingrid. She was, now that I thought of it, a definite Ingrid, not Ginger. What if Ingrid Bergman had been nicknamed "Ginger"? *Casablanca* starring Ginger Bergman. The idea was laughable.

"Ah, my sweet Ingrid," Uncle Gerald said, moving his rough hands over her back.

Mother nudged me and nodded sharply at the door. We left Uncle Gerald and Aunt "Ingrid" alone then. "You boys go to the movies or something," she said when we were in the kitchen. She gave William and me a half a dollar each.

"There's nothing good playing," I said.

"Go anyway," she said.

There was a Joan Crawford movie at the Variety. It was about a woman who kills her unfaithful husband by giving him gradual doses of poison. When her husband finally fell down dead in his study William said out loud, "Jesus, it's about time, hey?" We were thoroughly hushed by the people around us. We left the theater before the movie was half over. William cut a fart in the aisle.

"Gone with the wind," I said.

"Smoke gets in your eyes," William said.

"When Johnny comes farting home again, hurrah, hurrah," I said.

"You smell me your dream, and I'll smell you mine," William said.

A man leaned into the aisle in front of us. "Shut up, you morons," he said.

As we left the dark theater I heard a thunderclap. It was a storm—in the movie. I looked back and saw Joan Crawford dart for cover under some blowing trees.

When we went into the street, it was raining. It was one of those freakish summer storms that blow in from the Southwest taking southern California by surprise. The rain was tropical, the drops almost hot as they struck my skin. I was astonished. I looked at William but he hadn't made the connection:

—A thunderclap and rainstorm in the movie.

—Rain falling on Adams Boulevard.

"Isn't this weird?" I said.

"What? Isn't what weird?" William said.

I pointed back into the Variety. "There's a rainstorm in the movie, too."

"The Monk thinks rainstorms are weird," William said.

The rain came down hard, the big hot drops soaking through our shirts in seconds. The street jumped with the heavy downpour. I walked back into the theater. Since the movie was almost half over, no one stopped me. Joan Crawford was sitting behind the wheel of a car, her crazy eyes narrow and glinting as she tried to see into the rainy night. Her windshield wipers thudded back and forth. She was driving too fast. There was a nickel-plated revolver on the seat beside her. She picked it up and held it against her cheek, as if to cool a raging fever.

I went back out. William had started walking home. The downpour roared in the street. Then I remembered Uncle Gerald. He'd stood in a sprinkler, thinking it was rain. The coincidences were piling up. I sprinted to catch up to William. I grabbed his arm. Significance webbed the air, connecting everything.

"Here's something *else* that's weird," I said.

William shook my hand off his arm, kept walking.

"Your dad thought it was raining. He was standing in the rain but looking up at the stars."

"Monk."

"What?"

He stopped. He put his hands on my shoulders and held me at arm's length. "You're not just *crazy*, Monk."

"I'm not?"

"No. You're boring, too. You're boring the living shit out of me, Monk."

↓

The masts went up first. Uncle Gerald tied them into the corners of the guard wall with heavy galvanized straps which he spiked into the guard wall's studs. Then he nailed the guy wires down at strategic points on the roof. The guy wires had already been attached to the masts, midway up, as had been the beautiful copper wire of the aerial itself, which dangled down from heavy porcelain insulators high at the top of the twenty-foot trees. When all the guy wires had been tightened in place, Uncle Gerald raised the antenna wire by means of a rope-and-pulley arrangement. The pulley creaked as the brilliant, heavy-gauge copper wire rose off the roof and gradually tightened into a gleaming rectangle that was already alive with radio signals from the four corners of the world. From the middle of one side of the antenna, a single wire dangled down. It was covered with rubber insulation and was long enough to reach my bedroom window with several yards to spare. This was the lead-in wire I'd attach to my radio.

It had taken all morning and part of the afternoon to complete the project. Uncle Gerald sat down and opened a bottle of Ballantine. He offered me a swig. I started to decline, then accepted the bottle. I took several careful swallows of the warm, bitter ale.

The copper wire was no longer a mystery: He'd gone to a

junkyard and found four broken generators from old cars. The generators were full of heavy-gauge copper wire. I'd watched him patiently unwind the armatures. As he unwound the wire, I gathered it into coils the diameter of the length of my forearm, hooking each strand over my thumb and under my elbow. We had wire to spare. The trees still bothered me, though, and after another few swigs of ale I asked him about them.

"Los Angeles has a lot of fine parks, Tryg," he said. "And those parks have more trees than anyone knows what to do with. No one is going to miss a few saplings."

He opened another bottle of ale. "Let's celebrate," he said. He offered me first swig. The bitter taste didn't seem quite as vile this time. I looked up at my fine antenna. Malcolm's Revenge gleamed in the afternoon light. Actually, it wasn't just a simple rectangle of copper wire. Uncle Gerald had arranged it so that we could use as much of the salvaged generator wire as possible. Opposing corners of the rectangle were tied together by long wires. These wires made a giant **X** over the roof of the apartment building. It seemed to me that we *had* built a kind of net, a net that would trap any radio signal that fell out of the Los Angeles sky.

"Might I have a sip of that now, laddybuck?" Uncle Gerald said, reaching for the bottle.

We passed the bottle of ale back and forth. A wind had arisen out of the west and the antenna sang. An A T-6 roared over our heads, climbing steadily into the sun. I raised an empty ale bottle and sighted down its brown barrel at the plane.

Uncle Gerald took the bottle out of my hand and set it down. He sighed. "I'm very tired," he said. I didn't think he meant "sleepy." He opened another bottle. Again he gave me first swig.

"Did I tell you about my other wife, Tryg?" he said.

"The one that died in the car. Yes, you did."

"No, not Philly. The girl I married after Philly. Her name was Georgette West. She was an Eskimo woman. I met her in Juneau and we made love in the midnight sun. It was a short marriage, lasting but a few months. Short and deeply irrational, Master Trygve."

We were not on equal footing. But then, I also understood that he didn't expect me to respond. I sipped from the ale bottle. I couldn't distinguish the singing copper wire from the singing in my head.

"A certain kind of woman," Uncle Gerald said, "will put iron in your manhood." He glanced sharply at me. "I suppose I shouldn't be talking to you this way. I realize that. But then where else would you learn about such things? Who's going to tell you if not your uncle?"

I shrugged. But even that was too much of a response. The shrug assumed a willingness that wasn't there. This was my Uncle Gerald. He was married to my Aunt Ginger. He was old and his views of life were hammered out of raw experience. What could he tell me that I could possibly understand?

"Georgette was that kind of woman. There were two of us after her. She said, 'Fight for me. Go down to the floor for me.' She wanted a hero. Normally a man would say, Let the devil take her. Where does a woman like that get off, anyway? But she was different. Here was a woman you were glad to fight for. It was the only way, you see. So I fought a man. Then, by the end of summer, it was over. By the end of summer we hated each other. She punished me and I punished her. These things happen."

I nodded. I wanted to try out my antenna. I was dizzy and bored.

"Georgette West," he said nostalgically.

I sipped the ale, nodded wearily. I tried to picture the Eskimo woman, Georgette West. I couldn't. All I saw were igloos and fish. I couldn't imagine dying in the arms of such a woman while an orchestra played "The White Cliffs of Dover." I had a feeling that Georgette West didn't even know there was such a thing as World War Two. She was somewhere in Alaska asking men to fight for her. "Go down to the floor for me," she hissed in my ear. I refused politely. More important battles waited for me thirty thousand feet over the Pacific Ocean.

"I don't know why I brought all this up," Uncle Gerald said.

I shrugged and nodded. Uncle Gerald put his hand on the back of my neck and squeezed affectionately.

"No, no," he said. "You'll never have to deal with a woman like Georgette West. I can see that. In a way it's a shame, as well as your good fortune. I can see you're going to occupy yourself with the higher things. Well, good for you, lad. Good for you."

↓

"Remember Pearl Harbor." That was Malcolm's coded message. I finally realized that the numbers superscripting the letters divided the alphabet into five groups taken in order, and that the two even-numbered groups of letters were not altered at all while the odd-numbered groups were reversed in the same way as the simple code I'd taught to Jane Webster. I checked the mail each morning for a letter or card from Malcolm. I wanted his address so that I could send him an uncrackable message in code, but nothing came. William showed less eagerness for the mail, but I knew he was looking for a letter from Betty. Finally one arrived. It had no return address on it. William read it several times at the kitchen table, then crumpled it up and threw it into the garbage. I volunteered to take the garbage out to the incinerator that day. Before I tossed our bag of kitchen garbage into the big concrete burn-box, I fished out William's letter from Betty. "Dearest, dearest William," it said. "I'm going to be as frank with you as you would be with me. I met this boy, Barry, and we are very much in love. I love you and I always will. I'll never forget you, William. Can you believe me? It's true. I can't explain. There are no excuses for it. It just is. Do you understand? I know you do. It simply happened, and I know it will happen to you again, too. It will. Please don't think badly of me. I remain your loving, Betty."

I tossed the crumpled letter onto the piled sacks of garbage. Then I lit the mess. A white filament of smoke curled out of the chimney, followed by an angry black spume.

↓

My little two-tube radio had limited selectivity, and now that it was connected to Malcolm's Revenge, several stations competed for each setting of the dial creating a roar of heterodynes that sounded like the trumpets of Imperial Rome. Late at night, though, stations from the bottom of the world whispered in my earphones. The bells and chimes of Nepal tinkled in the nighttime calm of Los Angeles. The drums of Africa and the gongs of China thumped and reverberated, widening the sphere of my fantasies. I read an article in an amateur radio magazine about the sounds a meteor will make in the high-frequency shortwave bands. I plugged in my ten- and fifteen-meter coils and sure enough, if I waited patiently, the Doppler whistles and bursts that signified a meteor entering and ionizing the atmosphere rewarded me. During the meteor showers of mid-August, the whistles and grunts sounded like a legitimate invasion from outer space. And in between these meteor raids, I'd listen for hours, without a moment of boredom, to the constant cosmic hiss. The universe was a noisy place, blasting our world with constant messages in its indecipherable codes.

One morning, very early, I picked up Japan itself. Tokyo Rose was playing records for the GIs in the south Pacific, and in between selections, she'd speak to them. "Hi, GI Joe, what do you know? Or rather, what *don't* you know. I'll bet you *don't* know that you're fighting this useless war for the sole benefit of the Wall Street millionaires. Do you think Mister Roosevelt is one of *you?* Wise up, Joe." And so on. Her voice was smooth and her accent was perfect, except for a slip now and then. I wished her dead. I wished a B-25 Mitchell would drop a load of incendiary bombs on her radio studio. I saw myself delivering the lethal bombs. I had my crew bail out over the ocean because I knew this was a suicide mission. It was the only way. I brought the B-25 in low, over the rooftops, just like in the movie *Thirty Seconds Over Tokyo,* starring Spencer Tracy and Van Johnson. I saw the towers of the radio station and zeroed in on them. The station had big windows overlooking the city and I came in level with them. And there she was, holding a portable microphone in her hand, looking straight into my suicidal eyes. She was gorgeous, with her red silk kimono and black lustrous hair. The fear on her beautiful face froze my hand on the bomb release switch. I shook the image out of my mind and made another pass, forcing a cruder, more malicious face on the woman with the microphone. Then I released my bombs. I yanked back the wheel, knowing it was futility itself to try to outrun the fiery blast.

The second time I picked up Tokyo Rose it was mid-morning. I wanted someone else to hear her, but no one was around. William had gone to the beach by himself and both Mother and Aunt Ginger were at work. I walked around the apartment building, looking for anyone, but the place was deserted. The girl across the street was sunning herself on her lawn. I yelled at her from the curb. "Hey, you want to hear Tokyo Rose? I've got her on my radio." She looked at me with vague eyes, as if it were inconceivable that I had addressed her.

"Were you speaking to me?" she said, loftily.

"Yes. Tokyo Rose is on my radio, in person. Do you want to hear her? It's really ... *weird*."

She got up reluctantly, as if summoned by a parent. She ran a finger along the edge of her shorts, unsticking them from her sweaty, suntanned thighs as she crossed the street. She was wearing sandals and her toenails were painted coral pink.

She followed me into the apartment building. She walked slowly, in a practiced way. I recalled Mitchell's instructions and tried to stay as much as possible on the balls of my feet. *Balls first, balls first,* I told myself. Her languid ways and her pink toenails made me want to appear sophisticated, worldly. Her large breasts lifted her halter into jutting points.

I had to hold the door to our apartment open while she sauntered indifferently down the hallway, her lips pursed.

"It's cool in here," she said, glancing sharply around the apartment, evaluating it. "This is nice," she said.

"My radio," I said. "It's in my room." I led the way to the back bedroom.

I went in first and picked up the earphones and held one to my ear. It was filled with solar static and cosmic hiss. There was almost a voice in the background, but it was mostly my imagination.

"*This* is your room?" she said.

She had a thin, beaky nose; her eyes were small and suspicious. She held her lips in a constant, evaluating pucker. I began to think it had been a mistake inviting her over to hear Tokyo Rose. "Sure, it's my room," I said. "And my cousin's."

"Your cousin's the big Mexican kid?"

"He's not Mexican, he's Canadian."

"How very interesting," she said, meaning the opposite.

I searched for the voice of Tokyo Rose, earphones clamped to my skull. I sat down and worked the dials seriously. Navy stations were everywhere, clogging the bands with their interminable Morse code cryptograms. "Dammit," I said.

"No Tokyo Rose, huh?" the girl said. She stood behind me and yoked the back of my neck between her breasts. I hunched forward, out of their reach.

"I *had* Tokyo Rose," I said. "I had her coming in loud and *clear*, honest."

"What's so great about Tokyo Rose, anyway?" she said, nastily.

I looked at her. She grinned down at me, aware of my foolishness, certain of her own superiority. I took off the earphones. "She's not so great," I said. "It's just that she says such nutty things. I mean, she tells *lies*, basically incredible lies."

She stared dully at me, her lips pursed. "The human dictionary," she said. She sat on the bed and picked up a comic book. She paged through it without reading a word, then tossed it aside. "Where's your dumb cousin?" she asked.

"Out. At the beach. Venice, I think."

"Looking for girls, I bet," she said.

"I don't think so," I said. More than likely he was looking for a fight. He'd been more sullen than ever after Betty's letter. His dangerous look was on his face constantly.

I got up and walked around the bed toward the door. She grabbed my arm. "Hey," she said. "You never *had* Tokyo Rose on that crappy little radio, did you?"

My mouth went dry. "Sure I did," I said. "Really, but shortwave fades a lot. I mean, you can have a strong signal one minute, then the next minute it's gone, especially in summer."

"I think you're lying to me. You look like the kind of pill that tells a lot of lies."

"No, it's true," I said, but my voice was a dry whisper.

She put her other hand on my arm and yanked me down to the bed. I fell on my side, next to her, and she applied a leg scissors on me that crushed the air out of my lungs.

She rolled on her back. Her strong pelvis lifted me into the air. I was on top of her. She pulled my face down to hers, jamming her puckered lips into my teeth. Her pelvis rose and fell in powerful waves, lifting me high and hauling me down.

Then she rolled away from me and stood up. "What the hell do you think you're doing, you twerp?" she said. She tugged her shorts down on her dark thighs. She smoothed her hair. "I'm going to tell my dad what you tried to pull. He's a cop. L.A.P.D."

I was still on the bed, incriminated. "I didn't do anything," I whined.

"Hah!" she said into my face, the withering look in her small eyes promising vengeance. "I'm going to have you *whipped*. Liars like you ought to be *whipped*."

I escorted her to the door, hoping for a reprieve. I didn't get one.

When the news came that Uncle Gerald's ship had been torpedoed and that he, along with the rest of the crew, was listed as "missing at sea," Aunt Ginger accepted it as if the telegram were just a footnote to a well-known historical event. She read the telegram only once, then threw it away.

"Maybe he's on a lifeboat, and the PBYs haven't spotted him yet," I said. I felt it was my duty to offer encouragement.

"No," she said. "There wasn't any lifeboat."

A few days later we were at the kitchen table having our morning coffee. I'd developed a taste for it, provided it was diluted with cream and lots of sugar. Uncle Gerald's torpedoed ship was still on my mind. Aunt Ginger and Mother both looked haggard, as though they hadn't slept well.

"If they had to row, it might take weeks to get to Alaska," I said. "They could eat sea gulls and fish, like in the movie *Lifeboat*."

Aunt Ginger put her hand on mine. "You don't have to say these things, Trygve," she said. "I'm okay."

I realized then that I'd been offering these encouragements daily, ever since the telegram arrived. I slurped at my steaming cup.

"Jesus," Mother said. "You sound like a Norwegian farmer."

I looked into my cup, studying it. I tried to see the north Pacific, near the Aleutian Islands, where Uncle Gerald's ship had gone down. I tried to imagine being torpedoed, tried to see it coming through the eyes of Uncle Gerald. I could see the distant periscope cutting a thin wake, the angrier wake of the swift torpedo as it angled toward the fat hull of the freighter, but I could not imagine the impact, the shock and blast, the sudden funnels of fire and smoke, the terror, the screams of the wounded, or the dread realization that death was minutes away.

William came into the kitchen. He was still in his pajamas. His cheek was bruised under his left eye and his lip was cut. He'd received the news of his father's death with rage. He'd pounded the walls of our bedroom with his fists until the plaster cracked. Then he'd run out of the apartment, choking on the grief he would not give voice to. When he came in that night his shirt was torn and bloody.

"You can't run from it," Aunt Ginger said, reading my thoughts.

I looked up at her over the rim of my cup, but she wasn't talking to anyone in particular. "Gerald knew it as well as I did," she said. "It's a circle. You are its center and everything that happens goes around and around, bringing the same things back again. The burdens will be there, heavier or lighter."

William poured himself a cup of coffee. He said something

under his breath. Mother looked at him sharply. I sipped at my cup, trying not to slurp.

"Gerald will come back. I will come back. It will start all over again and it will end again."

"Only the names will be changed to protect the innocent," William said. His tone was bitter. He sat down next to me. I saw that the knuckles of his right hand were big and bright, the skin scraped raw.

"We all come back," Aunt Ginger said, saddened by William's remark.

"Like onions," William said.

We all looked at him. He belched. "Onions," he said. He tapped his stomach with the barrel of his fist and belched again. "Onions come back on you, too," he said.

I laughed at William's joke. "*Pepsi* comes back," I said. "*Coke* comes back." I tapped my stomach with my fist but failed to raise gas.

Aunt Ginger looked at me, her eyes dark with all the heart-break of human life.

"Shut up, Monk," William said. "I'm sorry, Ginger," he added.

I was thunderstruck by my own stupidity. Aunt Ginger blew her nose and I realized then that she'd been crying all along. I excused myself from the table and went out.

Emotions I didn't understand ran through me in crosscurrents. I went up to the roof and sat under the wonderful antenna my Uncle Gerald had built for me. It gleamed in the morning sun and the breeze made a low humming sound in the wires. I rubbed my eyes with the backs of my fists but they were dry.

A flock of birds landed on the wires of my antenna. They were joined by another flock. Soon the wires were sagging with gab-bling, disrespectful starlings who didn't have the slightest idea of what they were perched on. I ran around the roof under the massive **X** they made, flapping my arms, possessed by mind-blotting fury.

"Get off, you stupid shits!" I yelled. "Get off, you dirty fucks!" I screamed. The birds rose from the wires in a great, air-shaking whir.